CAITLIN MORAN is an award-winning columnist, interviewer and critic for *The Times*, as well as the author of the hilarious and provocative *How to be a Woman*.

The Chronicles of Narmo is her debut novel, written when she was just sixteen years old, and demonstrates the wit that has made her one of the most popular writers of the day. On publication, Terry Pratchett said "Oh God, this good already and she's only fifteen".

Also by Caitlin Moran

THE Chronicles OF Narmo

CORGI BOOKS

THE CHRONICLES OF NARMO
A CORGI BOOK 978 0552 57066 4

First published in Great Britain by Corgi,
an imprint of Random House Children's Publishers UK,
A Random House Group Company
Original Corgi edition published 1992
This Corgi edition published 2013

1 3 5 7 9 10 8 6 4 2

Copyright © Caitlin Moran, 1992

The extract on page 112 is taken from Bedknobs and Broomsticks by Mary Norton,
published by J.M. Dent & Sons Ltd. Reprinted with permission.

The right of Caitlin Moran to be identified as the author of this work has been asserted
in accordance with the Copyright, Designs and Patents Act 1988.

Our paper procurement policy can be found at www.randomhouse.co.uk/environment
Set in Adobe Caslon Pro
Corgi Books are published by Random House Children's Publishers UK,
61–63 Uxbridge Road, London W5 5SA

www.randomhousechildrens.co.uk
www.totallyrandombooks.co.uk
www.randomhouse.co.uk

Addresses for companies within The Random House Group Limited can be found at:
www.randomhouse.co.uk/offices.htm

THE RANDOM HOUSE GROUP Limited Reg. No. 954009

A CIP catalogue record for this book is available from the British Library.

Printed and bound in Great Britain by CPI Group (UK) Ltd, Croydon CR0 4YY

For Gillian Anne Rowley – who knew I couldn't be an actress, shouldn't be a ballerina, and that no-one could make a career out of being Nancy from Swallows and Amazons.

I wish you could have seen this.

Introduction

The thing is, once you've read a lot of books, you begin to think it might be time to just . . . write one of your own. That, you know. It's your *turn*. That you should *join in*. That books, and bookery, should be, ultimately, reciprocal.

At thirteen, I had read a lot of books. It was the third most-notable thing about me, after the fact I a) always wore a straw hat, the kind that donkeys wear at the seaside, and b) I had grown my hair down to my hips – which two facts conspired to make me look like illustrations of Cousin It from *The Addams Family*, attempting to shield myself from the sun.

I liked being pale. Having done all my research in books, I wanted to be as pale as a Moomin. As pale as the goats' cheese in *Heidi*, or the ice-splinter in Kay's eye in *The Snow Queen*, or the petticoats in Katy Carr's top drawer, in *What Katy Did*. As pale as the page in a book.

Every day, I put my hat on, and walked to the local library, and came back an hour later with a rucksack full of books. I read everywhere. On the floor, in the bath - in the car, until I was sick. Up the hazel tree in the garden, in the highest fork, fully six feet off the ground; until it became too dark, or cold, and I had to come inside.

I had even perfected how to read whilst peeling potatoes – wedging a book behind the mixer tap, and getting dinner ready whilst walking through Narnia, or Fantasia, or Mordor.

I had a list of all the books I'd read, by my bed: 311 fiction books, and 390 non-fiction. It would have been double the number in both lists, but I'd nobly discounted every single book I'd read whilst at junior school, as being "too easy." So, no *Faraway Tree*; no *Mallory Towers*. No *Family At One End Street* – those beginner books, from the lower shelves of the library. Just straight in with *The Railway Children* and *Anne of Green Gables*; the James Herriots, Spike Milligans, Terry Pratchetts, and *Gone With The Wind*.

I had adjudged which books were for the more "mature" audience by the print-size – which, I had noticed, invariably became smaller as the target demographic became older. Whilst *The Faraway Tree* was in a simple, round, eight-year-old-encouraging 22-point, *All Creatures Great &*

Small was in a much more business-like 14-point – presumably to keep the volume slimmer, and easier to fit in the pocket of a busy veterinarian.

Gone With The Wind, meanwhile, was in a retina-damaging 10-point, close-printed, on tissue-like paper so thin that, if you pressed it hard, you could read the next page through.

To compound the retina damage, I would read by the "night-light" – a string of 15 multi-coloured fairy-lights, left up from Christmas. By their dim rosy magic, I caned off all the Brontes in less than a week, squinting, and fast-tracked myself to a massive pair of NHS glasses, which, as I dolorously noted in my diary, "Make me look like my name is Alan."

And so, at 13, in a scholarly pair of glasses that made me look like Alan, with 601 small-print books theoretically in my head, I decided to write a book of my own.

"It's time I started paying back," I thought. "It's time to switch from 'reader' to 'author'."

Here are all the things I didn't know when I started to write my book – this book – in July, 1988.

1) That you cannot write a book in a day. This was a massive blow to me because, at the time, I fully believed you could. After all, it only took me a day to read a book – so it must, surely, follow that it took only a day to write one?

I sat down, at 10am, with a cup of cocoa and a strawberry jam sandwich, and started writing the first page: pencil on ruled A4. My presumption was that when I finally rose again – perhaps some time after 6pm – I would have my first novel, wholly complete, in my hand.

Looking up some time later, I was astonished to see that it was 11.04am – at which time I had generally presumed to be hitting Chapter Four – and yet I had filled only two sheets in my WHSmith Value Pad. How could this be? How could I be so far behind on my schedule? I hadn't even taken any breaks to play with my magnetic chess set which I was, at the time, obsessed with. I had eschewed even the toilet, as I presumed the really hard-core writers – Charlotte Bronte, and Jilly Cooper – did.

Working on the presumption that, in order to make more stuff – words – come out, I would have to put something *in*, I made another three jam sandwiches, and knuckled back down to work. That, I thought, should be enough calories to get to Chapter Two at jet-speed.

When I looked up again – dazed and shaky from effort, and also still slightly sticky from jam-residue – it was just 11.47, and I'd written 101 words, plus completed a massive doodle of a cat wearing a top hat, like that of Slash from Guns'n'Roses.

I started to realise that my initial plan – to write between fifteen and thirty books a year – might need a bit of a re-think.

I eventually finished the book in the summer of 1990 – two years later. Half of this was because of:

2) As the author, it's enormously helpful to know how a book ends *before* you start writing it. And, indeed, who's in it. Good to have some characters, and stuff, by the time you get onto that chair.

Again, I'd learned all I knew about writing from reading. At the beginning of books, the author very rarely, if ever, says, "I know everything that's going to happen in this book! I have PLANNED IT ALL! I know ALL THESE GUYS! Check

THIS meticulously plotted stuff out!"

To me, as a reader, they just seemed to be kind of . . . writing down things as they happened, instead.

This was, I presumed, because they were only finding out what happened at the same time as the reader, ie: that they were making it up as they went along. I basically thought some manner of omniscient god-librarian dictated all books – perhaps even autobiographies – to authors, and all authors had to do was sit quietly at their desks and write it all down, like peasants standing under a fruit-tree holding out a hat, waiting for the plums to fall.

I sat, quietly and obediently, at my desk, waiting for my book to arrive from the sky.

By the spring of 1991, I was still waiting. I finally got very, very angry, and started having to come up with a book myself – based on things that had happened to me, and people that I knew, very thinly disguised – which I did in a massive welter of resentment, and petulance.

"I will show YOU, librarian-god whose non-existence I seem to have just proved to myself!" I would fury, from inside a fortress of jam sandwiches on the desk fully fifteen inches high. "I'll write the whole thing MYSELF, and THEN you'll feel sorry! Screw you, empty sky. SCREW YOU. I'M GOING SOLO!"

3) When you've finally finished writing a book – which you will truly believe almost destroyed you – you then have to read the book. And what you have to do then is take massive fistfuls of words – whole sentences that you remember being as painful to write as earache, or bad measles – and just ... throw them away. You have to kill, and kill, and kill again.

When I began the editing process, aged 14, I was still a child.

"Mum!" I would wail. My mother was acting as my editor, at the time. She would put her red pen through whole pages of text, shaking her head. "Mum! That page took me a DAY to write! A whole freaking DAY! At my age, that's like one fifteenth of my ENTIRE LIFE! You can't PUT MY LIFE IN THE BIN!"

"If someone was deciding whether or not to buy this book by opening it on a random page and reading it, would you be happy for it to be *this* page?" she said. "Would you want to be judged on this? Would you put this on your *grave*?"

"Well, no – but there's a good bit on the next page," I said, trying to point to it.

"Well don't let this bad page stop people getting to the next good page," she said, wisely – throwing the page on the ground.

For the first two days of editing, I picked up every page she threw and put it back in again - tearful that she was rejecting what I'd so effortfully made.

By the third day, however, I realised she was right – and started pulling out bad words, sentences, paragraphs and pages myself, by the fistful, almost compulsively, like someone pulling clumps of moulting hair from a cat.

I ended that editing process an adult. Not because it went on for two whole years – although there were times, when we were arguing, that it felt like it did. But because there is something enormously fortifying about learning, early on, not to fear ripping it up, and starting again.

If you've never made anything before, you can be enormously protective of what small, new thing you do, and become quite defensive – and, therefore, ultimately limited – about trying to preserve it.

If you're having to burn stuff to the ground and rebuild every day, on the other hand, you soon start to assume the swaggering, misplaced confidence of a Ranger, such as Aragorn, or survivalist castaway, like Lucy Irvine in *Castaway*. However many words you bin, new ones will come, in their place. Better ones. You have nothing to fear. All you have to do is keep sitting down on the chair, and keep going.

4) Or, sometimes get off the chair, and keep going. When the book was finished, I laboriously typed it all into our computer, printed it out – 300 pages, double-spaced, like it said in the "Style Guide" in the *Writers' and Artists' Year Book* – and sent it off to five publishers; picked because, as the *Writers' and Artists' Year Book* suggested, they' d already published books I liked.

I stood in the Post Office queue with five vast bricks, wrapped in brown parcel paper, "London" written on them in thick black pen – my sum hopes and ambitions for the future; all the eggs in my basket - and spent a quarter of the family's weekly benefits on the postage.

"It's worth it," my mum said, bravely, as we prepared to semi-starve. "It's your big chance."

Within three weeks, four publishers had sent the manuscripts back – the saddest knock on the door ever. The postman handing back the fat packages like they were run-over cats he'd found on the road, outside. You could practically see the stiff tails, poking out the side. Dead cat books. Those books were dead.

"Thank you for considering us, but . . ." the covering letters started. I never got further than that. I cried as hysterically as I would at have someone blowing up all the rail-lines and motorways out of Wolverhampton, and telling me I would have to stay here forever, and never live in London, where I planned to grow three more inches, and become thin, and have a flat on Rosebery Avenue in Farringdon. I had seen the road in the *London A-Z*, when I was planning my future meticulously. That was another book from the library I'd read in a day. The *London A-Z*, with all the churches listed, in the back, for those lost, and needing to pray.

But the fifth . . . the fifth publisher called, a

month later. Called on the phone, while the whole family gathered on the stair behind me, stacked like a gap-mouthed choir.

They called from London with my manuscript in front of them – staring at my pages. Reading them. Making me an author, because they were a reader, reading me.

When I finally put the phone down, there was a silence.

"They want it!" I said, finally. "They want it! I am a writer! I am a writer! I wrote a book!"

I was fifteen. I got a cheque for £1500, and spent it on bunkbeds, and a new hat, and books. Books that I bought in a bookstore – just like you could buy mine, now.

I was fifteen, and a reader and writer. I could do both of the things.

Contents

CHAPTER ONE

'Twas Two Days After Christmas, and All Through the House, Everyone was Bored, Including the Mouse . . .

The day after Boxing Day.

Lots of sales start.

Lots of sales end.

The broken Supero-Constructo-Set fragments are thrown away. The only crackers left in the cracker tin are those horrid water biscuits.

Morag Narmo shuffled downstairs in the tatty red dressing gown that had possession of her body most of the time, and started rifling through the

1

rest of her family's Bumper-Festive-Choco-Sick-Packs for Curly Wurlys.

The only inflated balloon left on the ceiling collapsed with a sad little sigh. A tin foil Father Christmas dropped off the Christmas tree with a dejected rattle.

Morag snorted at the lack of Curly Wurlys and took a Big 'n' Puffy marshmallow from her sister Lily's compendium instead. She sat on the sofa and followed the pattern on the carpet with her toe. Mud, the cat, wandered over and sharpened her claws on Morag's leg. Morag stared at her blankly.

'I'm bored,' she told Mud. 'Bored bored bored. The holidays are too long and my boredom threshold is too low.'

Morag is fifteen and, in the words of one misguidedly tactful person, 'rather spacious in the body area'. Her hair is the shape of a frightened yak's, and the colour of drowned mice. She wants to be famous but hopes she won't have to do anything too strenuous before she acquires large wodges of cash and her own TV station. Her attitude to life is 'Sod that'.

Lily swept into the room and sat as far away

as possible from Morag. She flicked an invisible speck from her lap and turned to her sister.

'Good morning, Morag,' she said, with brittle friendliness.

'G'mornin', Lily,' Morag answered, hiding the stolen chocolate under a cushion.

'I know you have my marshmallow,' Lily said, carefully polishing a fingernail on the edge of her dressing gown, 'but I shall merely ask you to put it back in my box later. I rise above argument.'

'Oh,' Morag said, nonplussed.

Lily started to polish the adjacent fingernail.

Lily is wearing something pastel, as usual. On an average day, Lily resembles a scoop of melted Neapolitan ice-cream, To continue the ice-cream analogy further, Lily sees herself as the '99' stick the world whirls around. Lily's chances of becoming the richest and best-loved actress in the world, her dearest dream, are about as substantial as the chocolate coating on a cheap choc-ice. At fourteen, Lily is a year younger than Morag: blonde, pretty, smug.

Carol wandered into the front room, humming absently. 'Hello, Mum,' Morag said, looking up and grimacing.

'What's the matter?' Carol asked, walking over to Morag, scooping up the cat as she went and kicking a few stray toys out of her way.

'Post-Christmas-Boredom,' Morag grumbled.

'Oh well,' Carol said, sitting down next to Morag, accompanied by a small sub-sonic marshmallow death-squelch. 'There's always dinner to look forward to.'

'Yeah,' said Morag, unenthusiastically.

Lily leaned over to Morag. 'You owe me a marshmallow,' she hissed.

Dinner-time rolled round with sullen inevitability, and so did the turkey, for the third day in a row.

It was starting to look mopey, and rather fed up with the whole idea of being a turkey. Who can blame it? Its entire cooked life had consisted of being groaned at, half-heartedly picked at, and shoved swiftly back into the fridge. The turkey didn't like its fridge-mates, either – several unsavoury characters.

It shared the top shelf with a rather militant bottle of French mayonnaise, a hardening piece of racist cheese and a tin of rusting cling peaches.

The salad drawer was occupied by a rather sad-looking coconut which was constantly picked on by the free-range eggs that roamed the lower reaches of the fridge, demanding protection money.

Morag looked warily at the turkey. It looked back. Morag shuddered and pulled it out of the fridge. The rest of the Narmos gave a half-hearted cheer as she carried it to the table.

Poppy Narmo, the youngest, is sitting in the chair next to Morag, bolstered up with a cushion and trying to bite Mud, the cat, who is eating her food. Poppy does not like cats; they are sneaky and devious and untouchable, and Poppy rather hoped she'd cornered that market some time ago. She has several points in her favour: huge blue eyes, innocent pink and white face, pudgysome cheeks, and a wee cherry nose. Throughout her two-year sojourn on this planet, the fates have smiled down on her golden curls. She does whatever she wants.

Poppy knocked a glass of pop over Lily, and a lot of shouting began. Morag took sides against Lily and accused her of being almost illegally stupid; not able to claim a one-track mind. Not even a small muddy footpath.

Aggy, in comparison, has a great big motorway of a mind, with thousands of well-appointed service stations and a relatively low litter problem. She's twelve; short, quiet, wears a small pair of granny glasses, and is the human equivalent of a fluffy little bunny rabbit. The sort of bunny rabbit that reads Baudelaire and formulates new theories about the universe. Whilst washing up.

Josh joined the Poppy Defence League and cited a very old argument that he brought up every time a family dispute occurred. The Saga of Josh's Stolen Purple Rubber Dinosaur was regurgitated six times a week on average.

Morag once described the annoyingly slim Josh as resembling 'a fistful of demented pipecleaners'. Josh never walks when he can run, and never runs when he could fall over and slide along on his head. He is nine years old, but since he exists at such great speed he can only remember about five of them. His hair is the colour of semi-burnt toast and resembles a dead creature-thing on look-out.

Lily called Morag 'Mrs Forth Bridge Hips'.

Morag eyed the gravy boat in a sneaky kind of way.

Bob and Max, the two permanent dogs of a

floating animal population, are sitting under the table, licking up the just-spilt gravy and avoiding Josh's absently kicking legs. Bob's appearance is reminiscent of a walking hairy sofa. Max's distant relatives were probably camels; or incontinent donkeys.

And then the inevitable point in the argument was reached; the part that every child recognizes. The parents wade in and start finding people to shout at.

Bill and Carol can be described together; they are parents and as such are fused at the brain.

Bill is tall, resembles an undernourished clothes horse, and writes verses for Christmas crackers and greetings cards. Milton he is not, unless we mean the disinfectant. His hair is on the wispy side, and his temper on Permanent Fray. He is either waxing long and exceedingly lyrical about the world and its failings, or slumped on the sofa reading or watching the telly. Carol tripped over him in Brighton as he was slumped on the beach watching the sea, spilt a paper cup of tea over him, and things just blossomed from there.

Carol is small, plump, and has a shortish honey-coloured perm that always looks just ready to be

renewed. Carol's most frequented emotion is Guilt:
Guilt because she might make her children too
dependent on her; Guilt because they might become
estranged chat-show hosts; Guilt about Bill; Guilt
about the dogs; Guilt about the cat; Guilt in case
she is getting a Guilt Complex and will become
a burden. She has a weakness for sit-coms with
vicars in.

'—fault, Morag, you should have stopped them.
Now go to bed! I don't want to see you.'

Morag trailed upstairs despondently, gravy
dripping off her hair and on to her shoulders. She
flopped on to her bed, and Bob, the dog, started
to lick her sympathetically. And also because he
was hungry.

The rest of the Narmo children squeezed on
to the bed around her.

'Parents!' Morag said in disbelief, wiping a
persistent gravy lump from her eyebrow and
flicking it in the general direction of the bin.
'They don't seem to understand, don't seem to
grasp that we are not just ordinary children. We
are Gonks, a proud and noble tribe. We have our
own rules, our own honour, our own song that

no-one can remember the words to. They can't boss us around like that.'

'Um, they can,' Aggy said, taking off her glasses and polishing a stray and badly aimed drop of gravy from them. 'They're bigger than us and they know what all the knobs on the stereo do.'

'But they can't just send us to bed,' Morag said, pulling out her battered straw hat from underneath Lily. 'It's just too demeaning.'

'They only sent you to bed,' Lily said, picking up one of Morag's magazines and flicking through it distastefully. 'We followed because we were hoping to crow a bit, rub it in, get smug, that kind of thing.'

'Oh,' Morag said. 'I see.'

'But I don't think we'll bother,' Lily continued, standing up. 'I think we'll go and play pontoon, enjoy our freedom.' She and the rest of the Gonks filed out of the room, laughing with exaggerated merriment.

Morag stared at the carpet and started to trace the pattern with her toe.

'I'm bored,' she said. 'Bored bored bored.'

CHAPTER TWO
The Narmos Get Radical

Several days later. Too late for any decent Christmas TV programmes, and too early for any New Year fare.

'Mum, are you worried about totalitarian authoritarianism?' Morag asked, leaning against the draining board with a bowl of cereal in her hand.

'No. Should I be?' Carol asked, scraping the jellied turkey bones on to a sheet of newspaper and making a neatish parcel of it all. The turkey sighed with relief. At last it was being laid to rest. The last few days had been a limbo.

'Yep,' Morag said, mashing spoonfuls of cornflakes into a soggy lump. 'Because totalitarian authoritarianism forces me to wear a very unsuitable uniform and share a classroom with thirty-one potential chicken pluckers five days a week when, quite frankly, I'd rather be floating pizza-boxes on the lake.'

'You don't want to go back to school next week?' Carol asked, rubbing her eye with her wrist.

'Right.'

'Are you being teased?' Carol asked, throwing the bone-parcel in the bin and wiping her turkey-greased hands. 'Are you being victimized or bullied or isolated in any way?' Carol had listened to a radio agony phone-in the day before. 'Remember, you can trust me, I'm your mother.' She tried to hug Morag.

'*Prerff*,' Morag snorted, pushing her mother off gently. 'Bullied? Me? They're all too scared.'

'Of who?' Carol asked.

'*Lily!* Who do you think?' Morag said with heavy sarcasm. '*Me*, they're all scared of *me*. Anyway, we're straying away from the original point a bit.'

'Which was?' Carol asked.

'School. I do not want to go there. It's

restricting and limiting and not-very-nice and—' Morag tried to think of a few key sixties words that her mother might respond to '—very unkarma-ific and a bad trip, er, man.' This seemed to do the trick.

'And how do the other Gonks feel?' Carol asked.

'Oh, they hate, loathe and despise school,' Morag announced cheerfully. 'They'd all rather feed their heads into waste-disposal units than do the academical.'

'Wasn't that a dance?' Carol mused.

'What?' Morag asked, nonplussed.

'The Academical. "Do do do the Academical,"' Carol hummed. 'Fred and Ginger did it in *Flying Down To Rio*, I think.'

'No wonder her surname was *Rogers*,' Morag said, wilfully misunderstanding. 'But we're still wandering down Sidetrack Lane. To put it as simply as possible, why do we have to go to school? Our little home is such a nice place—'

Carol looked at Morag with amazement.

'—all us Gonks would get to know each other better, be friendly and harmonious if we saw more of each other—'

Carol looked at Morag with disbelief.

'—and we'd be able to help you around the house with little tasks such as, um, looking after Poppy, and, um—' Morag looked desperately around the kitchen. Her eyes lighted on the dough. 'And making bread.'

Carol started to say something sarcastic to Morag, but stopped as a rosy-golden vision appeared before her eyes: all the Narmo children laughing merrily around the fireplace, eating hot rolls made by Morag, singing nursery rhymes to Poppy, and drawing little bunny rabbits on to the biggest Mother's Day card in the world. A caption entitled the scene, 'First In The Series Of Unrealistic Mothers' Dreams', but Carol was hooked.

'Mum?' Morag was saying, pushing her elbow impatiently. 'Mum? What do you say? Is it a brilliant idea or is it a brilliant idea?'

'We'll see,' Carol said, with a note of hopeful conviction. 'We'll see.'

Carol was woken the next morning by Poppy, clad only in an Ewok T-shirt and sweatband, jumping up and down on her stomach shouting, 'Snoe, snoe!'

'Uh, has it snowed?' she asked Poppy blearily.

'Yus,' Poppy said, giving her angelic grin. 'I dow out?'

'I'm not moving,' Carol said, tucking the duvet around her more tightly.

'I wot to go,' said Poppy, furrowing her brow. Then she gave a happy, wistful, soft-focus little smile, 'Daddy dow out wi me.'

'Daddy's asleep,' Carol said with a high degree of certainty, turning over. The next thing she heard was Bill shouting in pain.

'Daddy wake up now,' Poppy said happily.

'She's pulling my bloody nostril hairs out,' Bill shouted, clamping his hand over his nose.

'Just take her out in the snow,' Carol coaxed, wriggling further down the bed and closing her eyes. 'It's all she wants.'

'She wants a good smack on the bottom if you ask me,' Bill said, slightly muffled as his hand was still over his nose.

'No I not,' Poppy said indignantly.

'Bill,' Carol wheedled, 'you'll take your youngest child out in the first sparkling, virgin-white snow of the year, won't you?'

'No,' Bill said. 'Why should I?'

Carol tired of persuasion, and showed him exactly why under the duvet.

Bill yelped, rolled out of bed with the duvet still draped about his shoulders, and started to get dressed. There was a brief scuffle as Carol recaptured her stolen bedding; and an even briefer scuffle as Bill good-naturedly tried to smother her with his socks. He relented, sighed, picked up the now smug Poppy, newly clad in a maternity bra and a pink leg warmer, and carried her downstairs.

Carol tried to go back to sleep in the new-found silence, but a thought, the size of a walnut, rolled into the back of her skull. Carol focused on it slyly, sideways, so it shouldn't be startled and hop away.

She identified it.

School: The not going of.

In the very early days of Flower Power, just after people started respecting plants and just before they started smoking them, Carol had cherished visions of being Earth Mother extraordinaire; nurturer of children, worshipper of cats, wearer of the widest bell-bottoms in all of Southern England. But with the advent of Bill, and the passing of flares, these dreams had been mislaid. Now they returned with a vengeance.

Bill, who had come downstairs, realized how cold it was and decided to stay inside whether Poppy liked it or not. He was now comfortably ensconced in a plumpfy chair by the fire, reading a book about a spy.

Always assume, unless told otherwise, that when Bill is reading it is something that involves sex, drink, violence and clichés, all in pretty large doses. It usually has the title and the name of the author in shiny red writing on the front. This is so that people who dislike that kind of book can identify and avoid them.

Back to Bill, and Poppy, and Bill's book, who are respectively sitting, sleeping and being thumbed. This idyllic scene was shattered by the entrance of Carol, in a nightmare-pink wincyette nightie, waving a tattered newspaper cutting in the air.

'Carol, Carol, what are you doing?' Bill asked, wondering whether it was important enough for him to put his book down, or indeed use a question mark.

'Look, it says here, somewhere . . .' Carol said,

scanning the article. 'Ah-ha, here it is … That we, blah blah blah, have the right to educate our children at home. Look!' She thrust the cutting at Bill.

'What?' Bill grunted, wishing Carol would just go away.

'I've decided. It's the pumpbag that did it,' Carol said, eyes shining. 'We, Bill, are going to take the children out of school and teach them at home.'

'Why?' Bill said, as simply as he could.

'To give them a chance to blossom, to grow,' Carol said, spotting a slight opening for a bit of oration. 'I mean, for the first sixteen years of a child's life it's shut in a building that's falling down, understaffed, without even a bottle of milk and a soggy straw these days to sustain it; and then it has to write in books about dull things that have no bearing on life whatsoever—'

'Mmmm,' Bill said, as soothingly as he could.

'—you have to go out on to a muddy field whether you like it or not,' Carol continued, recalling her own school days, 'get your knees red raw, catch a ball in the eye, and then shed your games clothes in front of the rest of the class, trying to cover the more explicit bits with a pumpbag. You're rationed to one pencil a week, and if that breaks you have to write with your nose dipped in ink for five days—'

Carol was exaggerating a little here, but we catch her drift.

'And all this for at least sixteen years, with an option to stay on for another three at university! Mendelssohn peaked at fifteen, Mozart had an opera under his belt at twelve, Shirley Temple had a full count of curls at six. What else *can* we do but take the Gonks out of school?'

Carol was proud of her speech and saw a glowing future in world politics, or perhaps inventing slogans for T-shirts.

'Oh.' Bill was on firm ground now. He put down Carol's cutting and flicked to the right place in the spy novel. 'That's all right then.'

Carol stared at him. 'What do you mean, "Oh, that's all right then"? I just said we're taking the children out of school. I've just planted the seed of a plant that could either bear fruit or die and sort of mould where it stands, all covered in blackfly and stuff. Aren't you going to say something along the lines of "Wow"?'

'Nope.' Bill couldn't remember if Logan had just flown to Tahiti or just left it. 'Y'see, every so often you come to me with your hair sticking up and your nose all red and usually wearing something silly—' he gestured to Carol's nightie, '—and you say something like "Let's sell everything we've got, buy a Winnebago and tour Australia!" or "Let's trade the Cortina in for six horses and ride all round the British coast!" I'm not holding my breath.' He glanced down at the page and noted the word 'nipple'. Carol had no chance.

'This nightie,' she tried ineffectually, 'was an anniversary present from you.' Bill was in Tahiti and didn't hear.

'Well then,' she said, drawing herself up to her full height. 'I'll see what other, more supportive members of my family have to say.'

'Mmmmmmm,' said Bill, but it was debatable why.

'Right then. Right, then. Right. Then.' Carol left the room, tripped, and wished Bill could at least remember what size she was.

CHAPTER THREE
Cordon Bleurgh

Two weeks later, as Carol was writing a letter to the Education Authority asking for the Gonks to be deregistered from school, Morag approached her mother.

'I'm bored,' she said, perching on the arm of Carol's chair. 'There's nothing to do, nowhere to be.'

'I feel my children will find a new quality of life being taught at home,' Carol wrote. *'At school the curriculum falsely satisfies their natural thirst for knowledge; a kind of academical junk food. And—'*

A small scream from the hall signified the start of a brief tussle between Josh and Lily.

'—*taken out of what is, after all, an artificial environment, I feel their personalities will have a chance to blossom and bear fruit*—'

'—hope you get stung by a killer bee and die—'

'—*one of which will be more harmonious inter-familial relationships* – What is it, Morag?' Carol asked with slight irritation.

'I've been forcibly relocated to Boredom City,' Morag whined. 'Why did you take me out of school?'

'Whoaa there, whoaa just a minute,' Carol said. 'You were dead keen to leave school a few days ago.'

'I didn't know how utterly dull it is being at home,' Morag explained. 'Why don't we *do* anything around here?'

'"*We*" includes you,' Carol snapped. 'Why don't *you* do something? I'm afraid I'm just your mother, not a cross between P. T. Barnum and Disneyland. If you want anything to happen, you have to do it yourself.'

Morag crossed her eyes and feigned death.

'The truth hurts, Morag,' Carol said calmly, picking up her pen again. 'Now, this is a letter asking the Education Authority for you to be deregistered. If you want to return to school, where the amusement is laid on for you whether you like it or not, I'll rip this letter up and that'll be that. But if you want to make your own amusement, when you like to, where you like to, with no restrictions save those laid down by the Geneva Convention, go away and do something.'

Morag was still on the floor. She gazed up at the ceiling. School, or her own amusement. Those were the choices. Did she like herself enough to become her own best friend? Did she want enough time to 'find out who she was'? And if she did 'find herself', what if the Real Morag was the self-centred, bombastic, overbearing, but really quite lovable person she'd always suspected she was? Would the two Morags get on well?

'Better than having to get on with double maths and Mr Emikson,' Morag decided, shuffling out of the front room.

Carol smiled as she left.

'Something to do,' Morag sighed. She was slightly surprised to find that she'd wandered into the kitchen. 'Something to do. Bread, bread.

Making bread is something to do. And making it without a cookbook takes it on to a higher plain of "doing" entirely.'

She took the mixing bowl out of the cupboard and stared at it. Lily had washed it up last and there were blobs of bread dough cemented to the bottom. Morag sniffed them carefully.

'Flour,' she said. 'Water, salt, fat, small smears of Fairy Liquid. Should be easy.' Morag emptied a large bag of flour into the mixing bowl, threw a handful of salt in, and a generous amount of water. She stirred the goo. After about three minutes the mixture claimed her spoon, and Morag was loath to get it back.

'You want a spoon, you eat a spoon,' she muttered. 'It's none of my business. Probably make you grow big and strong.'

Morag went over to the cutlery drawer: a place where anarchy reigned supreme, and where the nasty silver-plated forks ate the baby teaspoons. She fetched a fish-slice and used it to heave the mess in the bowl around.

'Fat!' Morag said, slapping her forehead. 'Forgot the fat.' She rifled through the cupboard and found a bottle of olive oil. 'Perfecto.' Morag carefully measured two tablespoonsful into the bowl and then, thinking it didn't look right, tipped the bottle upside down and sloshed the rest in. 'Now we're motoring!'

The oil wouldn't mix in, and Morag couldn't help but think the dough didn't look quite right. For a start, it shouldn't have the look of a six-week-dead pig skin, and secondly, Morag was sure she'd read somewhere that bread dough was supposed to rise. The *thing* in the mixing bowl wasn't rising. She rubbed a bit of flour from her waistcoat and went into the front room.

'Mum,' she said, 'I'm making bread and it isn't rising. It' s kind of, well, sulking.'

'Yeast?' Carol said, in a mother-knows-best voice. Morag slouched back into the kitchen and wandered around, muttering 'yeast' in much the same way she wandered around muttering 'string' or 'Sellotape'. The cupboard doors were flung open.

'Yeast?' she asked the shelves, expecting the jars or bottles or packets or whatever-it-came-in to leap foward playing trumpets, waving banners and squeaking, 'Here we are, Morag.'

All remained silent.

Morag half-heartedly looked through the cupboard, and knocked a packet of cornflour over into a spilt puddle of marmalade. She wondered absently if that was how blancmange was invented. A small sachet of dried yeast came to light under the Marmite lid, and Morag, who couldn't be bothered to look for the scissors, tried to open the packet with her teeth.

Mistake.

The packet stretched to an inordinate length and then snapped, showering yeast all over the floor. A small piece of plastic packet rebounded back into Morag's mouth. She choked, and looked at the floor. Pity to let all that expensive yeast go to waste . . .

She tucked her hair into her collar, got down on her hands and knees, and looked under the sink unit. The dustpan and brush were hiding behind a spinning top, a copy of *Woman's Weekly* and a potato. Morag took the dustpan and brush out, taking care not to touch the potato, pulled a bit of chewing gum off the bristles and started to sweep up the yeast, and, for that matter, anything else that was on the floor.

*

A hygiene imp who was sitting on top of the fridge shuddered and dissolved.

When the dustpan was half-full, Morag emptied the varied contents into the bowl and gave it a cursory stir, stopping only to pick out a 'We Love Bognor' badge, give it a quick rub and pin it to her waistcoat.

Many miles away, Queen Effervescentmilton-tablet was holding court and listening to the tale of one of her scout hygiene imps, Washyourhands-beforeyoustart. She couldn't believe what she was hearing.

'*She did* what *with a potato?*'

'*L–l–left it there, your Royal Imperial Majesty-ness, ma'am.*'

'*In the dark?*'

'*Y–y–yes, your Clean and Tidy Neatness, ma'am.*'

'*Doesn't she know,*' *the Queen started,* '*that if you have a potato, and you leave it in the dark long enough, it'll come to life? And if you have a potato and a Woman's Weekly, you get—*' *The Queen trailed off.*

'*Yyyyy–you mean – your Royal Gargle with*

Undiluted Jeyes Fluid to Kill Every Single Germiness, ma'am?' the imp stuttered in horror.

'Yes. Another Barbara Cartland, I'm afraid,' the Queen admitted. 'I suppose, to avert this, I could summon a hero to go on a quest to warn Morag; solving riddles with mental dexterity, fasting in the Desert of a Thousand Seeds, that kind of thing, but—'

'Yes, your Royal Always Flush Before you Leave and Never Wipe Your Hands on the Curtain or the Person in Frontiness, ma'am?' the imp said eagerly.

'I just can't be bothered,' the Queen said. 'Sod Morag. Come on, let's go down the Duck and Diarrhoea for a quick half. Anyone else want to come?'

There was a general murmur of assent from her courtiers.

Back to Morag. And the Dough. And the potato, tragically left in the dark, and slowly mutating, although we won't dwell on it too long. Suffice to say it has just decided it likes Pink.

She poked the dough with the dustpan and gave a little squeak as it shuddered.

'This is definitely not good,' she muttered. 'Not good at all. I can't see Helen of *All Creatures Great and Small* giving this to little Jimmy with a bowl of soup and a glass of milk. Not even as a table mat.'

Morag couldn't find a red and white checked tea towel, which seemed to be a prerequisite in bread-making, and so settled for a pillowcase with Snoopy on. She was starting to leave the kitchen when Carol wandered in.

'Tidying up are you, dear?' she asked.

'Uh, yes,' Morag lied easily, grabbing the olive oil bottle and putting it back into the cupboard.

'That's what I like to see,' Carol said, scooping the cat off the sideboard and dropping it gently on the floor. 'Will we be having nice crusty bread for tea?' she asked, going to lift the pillowcase off the mixing bowl.

'Uh, I wouldn't do that,' Morag said, restraining her mother's arm.

'Why?' Carol asked.

'Uh, I just wouldn't,' Morag said, straightening the pillowcase. Carol seemed to sense the latent urgency in Morag's voice, and didn't question her.

'Well, I'll leave you to it,' Carol said, leaving

the kitchen with the cat trailing behind her.

As soon as Carol had gone, Morag threw all the mess into the cupboard under the sink and took one sweep at the sideboard with her arm, sending drifts of flour to the floor.

Then she threw on her coat and went for a very long walk.

CHAPTER FOUR

The Trip to the Zoo, and the Strange Creatures

It was a day in mid-February. The weather was fine enough to prompt thoughts of spring wardrobes, but too cold to actually wear them.

The Narmos were eating Morag's long-lived bread, which had been killed by severe toasting and buttering. This was breakfast, easily recognizable by the fact that no-one was talking. Bill was groaning, but this was because he'd had an Important Business Meeting in the Wheel and Clamp the night before.

Carol was combing through her ancient copy of *The Happy Hippy Guide to the Midlands*, and inserting her fingers between various pages to mark certain places. She had one digit left.

'We should go on an Educational Visit somewhere, Bill,' she decided. 'The children need to see new places, need to be infused with culture and alternative societies.'

There was an uninterested silence. Josh broke it eventually, partially because he was sorry for Carol, but mainly becasue he broke just about anything he could. 'Where should we go then, Mum?' he asked.

'Dudley Zoo!' Carol said.

There was an almost mutual familial rolling of eyes.

'Morally questionable—' Aggy started.

'Boring—' Lily continued.

'Too much walking—' Morag chipped in.

'I don't like it because they won't let you in the cages,' Josh complained.

'And it's too far away from the bathroom cabinet,' Bill added, swallowing another Rennie.

Carol turned to Poppy.

'Me want a *My Little Pony* video,' she said, by way of clarification.

Bill opened one red, bleary eye. 'So no-one wants to go,' he confirmed.

All the Gonks nodded in agreement.

'Well then, we'll just *have* to go,' he said, standing up.

'But you don't want to go either,' Carol said, puzzled.

'No, course I don't,' Bill said, starting to look better. 'But these Gonks have had weeks and weeks of doing what they want, being out of school. It'll give them a bit of thingy fibre to do something they don't want to. I can take the pain.'

The Gonks stared at him.

'Oh God,' Morag sighed.

*

'—forks, spoons, Marmite, rugs, spare clothes for Poppy, dog bowls, potty- Potty? Potty, Lily?'

'I can't find it,' Lily said breathlessly. 'I've looked everywhere.'

'But I have to tick it off my list,' Morag said, waving the list at Lily. 'The pot comes on every journey, that's why it's on my list of Essential Things. We've got to have it.'

Josh ran past. 'Peenie butter?' Morag asked.

'Check,' answered Josh, dumping it in one of the four large cardboard boxes by the front door.

'Coats?' Morag asked Aggy. In answer, Aggy pointed at the small coat-mountain that was blocking the hallway.

'I still can't find the potty,' Lily added.

'We have to have the potty,' Josh pushed in, 'or else Poppy'll have to wee in the Thermos cup.'

'Oh, stuff it,' Morag said wearily. 'Poppy can squat in a clump of nettles like the rest of us. Josh,' she added, grasping, him by the scruff of the neck as be ran past. 'Start loading these boxes into the car.'

Carol appeared in the doorway, vaguely waving a box of marked-down Kipling Mince Pies left over from Christmas.

'We could have a picnic,' she said, gesturing with them hopefully.

The Narmos sat in the car as Bill rooted around for the car keys – in his jeans and jacket pockets, fore, aft, left, right—

'Bill?' Carol said.

'Shush, Carol, please.'

—the little pocket in his T-shirt, the

secret compartment in his coat, the *un*-secret compartment in his coat—

'Bill,' Carol said, a little more urgently.

'Carol!' Bill growled.

—the zip on his hat, the turn-up of his jeans, the slot on his trainers where the leather hadn't stuck down, and all the various segments of his wallet.

He gave a bellow of frustration.

The Gonks shifted uncomfortably in the back of the car. One of the dogs started whining.

Bill slammed his hands down on the dashboard and followed suit with his head. He gave a roar of rage.

'Agggghhhhh, this is what I have come to expect from this family – one bloody cock-up after another! I mean, you do want to come out, don't you? So why is it left to me to run around like a blue-arsed fly, trying to pull heaven and earth together while you stand around like a bunch of lemons? I don't know why I bother, I really don't. I feel like calling the whole thing off. You do want to come, don't you?' he demanded of Josh.

'No, actually, no, we're here under protest,' Josh bawled back.

Bill sat for a minute. 'Carol, where are my keys?'

Carol got out of the car, walked around to Bill's door and took the keys out of the car-door keyhole. She dropped them through the window. 'Here, my love,' she said.

Bill wordlessly took the bunch, selected the right one, put it in the ignition, started to turn it, and—

'Me want a pee,' Poppy said. 'Me want potty.'

Morag looked at Lily. Lily looked at Morag.

Three-quarters of an hour later. A sullen, tearstained silence has taken over all the occupants of the car, save Morag. Her cheeks are bright pink from the stupendous argument she has just had with her father. It has involved several passers-by, a taxi-driver and a postman. The inquiry date is next Thursday.

Bill is now outside the car, fiddling with the aerial, head on his arm which is resting on the roof of the car. The car is a 1972 Ford Cortina Estate. It is hand-painted dark green, with acne scabs of Polyfilla. Everyone save Bill hates the car; but that will soon change.

The potty, now found, has been thrown into the next-door neighbours' front garden, where it resides lopsidedly on the head of a gnome.

Poppy is, very wisely, asleep.

Bill took a deep breath, kicked a piece of harmless gravel into the middle of the road where it could get hurt, and got into the car. One of the dogs tried to lick Bill; Josh restrained it, and went back to playing noughts and crosses on the steamed-up window.

Bill shut the car door, and the window fell down inside the framework.

*

Two hours later. The sun has now moved into Aquarius. Not that this influences anything.

Bill took a deep breath, the carbon monoxide from the bus over the road killing a few more brain cells. He gritted his teeth, snapped the aerial off, and got back into the car. He shut the door daintily, and sat quietly for a minute. Then he gave a weary smile, peered through the Sellotape holding the window in, brushed his hair back and turned the key in the ignition. Nothing happened. He gave a nervous laugh, and tried again. Nothing. He gave a little sob, and tried for the last time.

Nothing.

Bill gave a Wakaheiti death cry, kicked his shoe off, wacked the speedometer with it, got out of the car, banging the door as he did so. With a ripping sound the Sellotape divorced itself from the glass, and the window slammed back into the framework. Bill smiled a smile last seen on a piranha with toothache that has just eaten the last dentist in the Amazon, and kicked the car right in the hubcaps.

'That's it! That's definitely it! I hate this bloody car. No more!'

Josh poked his head out of the window. 'We're not going, then?' he asked.

'No.' Bill said shortly. 'We are not. I never wanted to take you out anyway. Go on, sod off back in the house.'

Bill threw the keys across the road, and Carol watched with an air of futility as they fell down the drain. The Gonks started to filter out of the car, carrying coats and cutlery. Morag dumped Poppy on a rug on the lawn. Bill opened the bonnet and stared morosely at the confusion of wires and tubes that dwelt there.

The dogs leapt out of the car and began to

bark, very loudly, at nothing. Poppy, having found an irritating ant and eaten it, was now pulling the wings off a moth, and laughing.

Bill used every swear word he could think of to describe the car, and ran out of abuse after five minutes. He wondered where the thesaurus was.

Then he started in French.

Mrs Vernon and Mr Gurney parked their car on the corner of Talcott Road and Rope Street, and walked around the corner. Mrs Vernon adjusted her brown wool skirt and looked at her clipboard.

'We're looking for number twenty-seven Rope Street,' she said. 'They were taken out of school last month, and this is our first visit ever. We have to assess the level of tuition, personal supervision, number of toilets per head, if they do projects about Romans, and if they know the names of three vegetable-eating dinosaurs. We need to know if there are any plans for school outings, if they intend to teach Islam in the dinner break, and whether they will give us any nice chocolate biscuits.'

'I do know, you know,' Mr Gurney sighed. 'I've been doing this for twelve years. After a bit the routine starts to sink in. You remember little things, like "Have they all got a pumpbag?" etcetera.'

'Yes, but Richard, don't you feel excited?' Mrs Vernon asked. 'It's the Midlands' first out-of-school experience, and we are the ones to see them first! We are making history! Up till now, all we've ever had to inspect are schools. Now we'll get an insight into a whole new way of life! Don't you have a little shiver going up and down your spine, like when Placido Domingo sings?'

'I can't say the overweight Italian has ever rendered my spinal cord wobbly,' Mr Gurney said, 'but I do agree this new project has certain, interesting, elements. Ah, what's this? Street theatre?'

Mrs Vernon looked up from her clipboard, and stopped dead. Outside the last house in the street, a man was hitting a dark green Ford Cortina with a spanner and screaming '*Merde!*' Three girls were unsuccessfully trying to catch two dogs, who were trying to chase one cat through a flowerbed. A skinny little boy was running up and down the path with boxes full of junk and dumping them on the front door step.

In fact, the only person acting normally was a small, angelic-looking two year old with a halo of golden curls, who was playing on the lawn and chuckling.

Mary Vernon pulled her brown wool hat down low over her ears, and approached the three girls.

'Uh, hello, dears,' she said genially. 'I was wondering, could you tell me where number twenty-seven Rope Street is, please?' Morag stopped shouting 'Heel!' and pushed her hair off her face.

'Are you from the rent?' she asked.

'No,' Mrs Vernon said, slightly surprised.

Morag screwed her eyes up. 'The Gas then?'

'No.'

''leccy? Phone?' Morag asked. 'TV licence? Give us a clue.'

'No, none of those, dear,' Mrs Vernon said. 'We're from the Local Education Authority. We've come to see the Narmos. Could you tell me where number twenty-seven is please?'

'Here,' Morag said simply, gesturing towards the house with its air of a permanent cringe, and heartily despised Roland Rat curtains billowing from Morag's open window.

'Are you sure?' Mr Gurney asked, figuring the amount of biscuits inside must be very small indeed.

'Yes,' Morag said. 'I'm Morag Narmo.'

Mary Vernon stepped forward. 'I'm Mrs Vernon, and this is Mr Gurney; we are your Inspectors. We thought we'd pop in and surprise you but, um . . . Where is your mother?'

'Um, looking down the drain. Don't ask me why.' Morag pointed over the road to where her mother was on her hands and knees, looking for the keys.

'Your father then?' Mr Gurney said, a trifle desperately.

Josh pointed at Bill, who was pulling the windscreen wipers off the car and had reverted to swearing in English. Morag winced. There would be trouble.

'Um, well, then,' said Mary Vernon, and marched resolutely over to Bill.

'Mr Narmo?' she asked.

'Yes?' he said, straightening up, with small bits of floppy rubber in his hands.

'I'm Mary Vernon, from the LEA. We understand that you are educating your children.

at home. We have come to see how they are getting along, and whether you have any drinking fountains.'

Bill stared at her.

'Oh,' added Richard Gurney, 'and I don't suppose you have any chocolate biscuits? You know the ones. In the blue packets. "One nibble and you'll be nobbled?"'

Bill stared at him, too.

'Um, would you like to come inside?' Aggy asked. 'We could watch *Home and Away*; you could have a cup of tea or something . . .'

'There's not much point if you haven't got any biscuits to dunk in it,' said Mr Gurney morosely.

'Oh, come on, Richard,' Mary said brightly. 'They might have some pictures or essays or something for us . . .' She looked at Morag hopefully. Morag shook her head.

'A cup of tea would be nice, in that case,' said Mary, still trying to remain bright. Mary tried to look on the bright side all the time, even if it meant rigging up arc lights in the Black Hole of Calcutta, metaphorically speaking.

'I'll put the kettle on then,' Aggy said, running up the path. She stopped at the front door.

'Who's got the front-door key?' she asked. All heads slowly turned towards Bill. 'Well?' he said, question, realization and defence all included.

'Where did you throw them, Dad?' Lily asked, wearying a little of sitting in the street looking delightfully provincial.

'Down the drain,' Carol called, straightening up from searching.

'At least Mum's venting her anger on the back gate,' Morag said to Aggy. 'Rather than us.'

'I'm trying to open it,' Carol snapped. 'Not break it. It's stuck.'

The Inspectors had joined the rest of the Gonks on the picnic rug with Poppy. The Gonks were telling the Inspectors their plans for the future. Well, that was how it started, but Lily's plans for the future had run for twenty minutes so far and showed no sign of ending.

'Give me a boost,' Carol asked Morag. 'It'll be quicker climbing over.'

'How are you going to get in the house?' Aggy asked.

'There'll be a downstairs window open around the back somewhere,' Carol said airily. Morag gave her a violent boost, and Carol disappeared.

Mrs Vernon smiled encouragingly at Lily.

'I've got the keys!' Bill shouted, who had spent the last ten minutes poking down the drain with the broken car aerial. 'We can go inside now.'

Carol was stuck in the kitchen window. Not just 'stuck' stuck, but stuck so that if she moved she would probably break her leg. Her other leg was resting in the sink in a very inelegant position. The tap was dripping on her foot. She idly resolved to fit a new washer.

'—come into the kitchen. We'll see if we've got any bis– Hello, Mum,' Morag said, with remarkable self-control, she thought.

The Inspectors stared at Carol.

'Um, come into the front room,' Morag said. 'And Aggy, help Mum.'

'. . . I say education? What is it? A collection of knowledge that continues throughout a person's lifetime? Or some finite, scheduled process that can be dealt with in a few crowded years at school? I prefer to think my children's *lives* are their education.'

Carol was just finishing an epic speech that had caused everyone's tea to go cold. Mr Gurney put down a small plastic wind-up penguin that didn't wind any more, and stood up.

'I see, Mrs Narmo,' he said, brushing down his trousers. 'Thank you for explaining that to us. I think we'll be on our way now. Thank you for the tea, Aggy. And lovely toast, Morag. Very, um, *interesting*.'

The Narmos waved the Inspectors goodbye from the doorway.

'Good stuff, that bread,' Morag said. 'It's got certain *qualities* to it. Anybody want some for dinner?'

The rest of the Narmos melted away.

CHAPTER FIVE

The Child, the Egg and the Wardrobe

Easter morning

The sun leapt through the window with a cheery 'Hey nonny nonny!' and noted the still sleeping Gonks. It sloped off, muttering about 'miserable somnolists' and 'could at least make an effort'.

Twenty minutes later, Josh opened his eyes and rolled out of bed. He brushed aside the Lego space-station he had landed on, and wondered if he dared to think about the Easter Bunny. If he did believe in Mr E. Bunny it would mean he was a baby and very gullible and stupid.

If he didn't, he wouldn't get any chocolate. Pride versus Greed. It was a nasty scuffle.

Pride kept harping on about how Josh was nine now and all that Bunny stuff was for Poppy and others of her ilk, but Greed won in the end after an on-the-belt blow, a quick telex from Josh's stomach.

Josh crept out of his room and proceeded at a Lego-injured hobble down the stairs. All illusions of Easter being for the kiddies were dispelled when he found Morag overturning sofas in the front room.

'Hello butt-features,' she greeted him.

'Hello, Mrs Wobble,' he said, lolling against the dresser. 'Didn't you spy on Mum last night and see where she hid them?'

'I tried,' Morag said grumpily, 'but by half past one she still hadn't done them and I fell asleep. We're actually going to have to look for them this year.'

'Oh, brilliant,' Josh said with heavy sarcasm.

'Well, you can either hunt for your egg,' Morag said, shoving the sofa back against the wall with her knees, 'or go chocolateless.'

There was a small pause.

'Have you looked in the dogs' beds?' Josh asked.

'Didn't think of there,' Morag said. 'C'mon, give us a hand.'

They ran off.

In order to reach the Earth, the Sun has to travel eighty million million miles, across the universe, through the atmospheres and magnetic pulls of countless planets; it has to seep its way through clouds of star dust twelve thousand miles thick. It plays leapfrog with time and has a neat little party trick of standing where it was eight and a half minutes ago And still – after all this exertion – it still had the energy to struggle through the yellowing nets and purple nylon curtains of Bill and Carol's bedroom, and wake them up.

'Oh Bill, Bill,' Carol moaned, sitting bolt upright and clutching her forehead in dismay. 'I didn't hide the Gonks' Easter Eggs. They're still in the wardrobe. What will my poor babies think of me? They're probably down there now, hunting and searching but to no avail, as they will never find their treasure. Oh Bill, what have I done?'

'You haven't done anything you silly cow,' the

semi-comatose lump beside her grunted. 'Go back to sleep.'

'But Bill, that's the point. I haven't done anything, and my poor children are—'

'Yes, I know,' Bill said, with his eyes still closed. 'Hunting and searching and digging and ruining sofas for fifty-pence-worth of chocolate in a cardboard box labelled "Six pounds please, suckers". Go back to sleep.'

'Bill, I can't. It's part of their childhood. I'm going down to hide them now.' Carol slipped out of bed, wrapped her dressing-gown around her, and opened the wardrobe door.

At the very bottom, where light did not usually fall, where matching belts for dresses dwelt in the dark morass, were ten crushed silver boxes. On top of the boxes there was a pile of multicoloured foil, shredded, making a bed for the small golden-haired child who lay curled up, her pink cheek resting on her chubby hand, eyes buttoned up in sleep. A large chocolate-coloured, chocolate smelling, chocolate-tasting ring circled her mouth.

'Poppy!' Carol gasped.

The child who answered to that name, when she felt like it, opened her eyes.

'Not me,' she said automatically.

'Poppy,' Carol said weakly, sitting down on the end of her bed.

Bill sat up. 'What's the matter?' he asked sleepily.

Carol pointed at the wardrobe.

'It's Poppy,' Carol said faintly. 'She's eaten all the Easter eggs.'

'*All* of them?' Bill repeated.

'Well, I doubt she missed any,' Carol said, sliding into annoyance.

'Well, call the Gonks then,' Bill said, sitting up in bed. 'We'd better break the news.'

Carol called the Gonks. Morag and Josh thundered up the stairs; Aggy and Lily trailed in from their room. They all stood lined up against the wall, shifting a little from foot to foot. Aggy didn't have her glasses on, and Lily stared pointedly at an unfiled nail.

Carol hauled Poppy out of the wardrobe. Poppy made a special point of being asleep and completely unwakeable. Carol woke her.

'Bad news, I'm afraid, Gonks,' Carol said.

She pointed to the empty egg boxes.

There was a pause.

'I not do it,' Poppy said, and then licked a bit of chocolate from around her face.

'Does this mean we aren't going to get an Easter egg?' Josh asked, on behalf of his stomach.

'Most probably,' Carol said, taking the empty egg boxes out of the wardrobe and stuffing them into the bin.

Morag went pale. Aggy blinked very forcefully. Josh gave a high-pitched wail that sent several devout Muslims to prayer.

'Well, I don't know why you're making such a fuss,' Lily said, winding a frond of hair around her finger. 'Y'all know chocolate is bad for you. We can have carrot sticks for breakfast instead. Yes, carrot sticks. It'll do your complexion the world of good, Morag.' Morag lowered her brows, but Lily had left the room.

'Aren't you going to buy us some more Easter eggs?' Josh demanded of Bill and Carol.

'Nope,' said Carol, as she and Bill crawled back into bed. Bill started to snore loudly. 'But that's not fair!' Aggy said indignantly.

'You can't do that, we'll be mentally scarred for life!' Morag added.

'Yeah, and what about my purple rubber dinosaur?' Josh demanded.

There was a silence.

'Not now,' Morag hissed. 'You'll dilute the essence of our argument. 'But it was too late. The Parents were asleep.

The Gonks filed out of the room indignantly.

That's it. End of chapter five. If Bill and Carol were lavish and bountiful parents they would have gone out and bought the Gonks replacement eggs. A jolly time would have ensued, with much merriment and laughter; all very reminiscent of the Waltons.

But Bill and Carol, unfortunately, were knackered, broke, and generally lacking in the boundless generosity department. The sun got very depressed about everything and sulked behind a cloud for the rest of the day.

But to return to Lily for a minute . . . She lounged on the end of her bed, listening to the rest of the Gonks clumping downstairs and talking very loudly about demonstrations next Father's and Mother's Days. Then, with a cool movement that exuded smugness, she took her

Emergency Easter Egg from underneath her bed. With a leisurely motion she unwrapped the egg and folded the bits of red foil into a pile. With a professional flick of the wrist, she snapped the egg in half and broke a piece of chocolate off. She held it for a while, turning it so its glazed surface shone. Then, just as it started to melt, she smiled and popped it in her mouth.

'Carrot sticks. *Pleurgh!*' she grinned.

CHAPTER SIX

The Off-White Wedding

Bill walked into the front room, flicking
through the junk mail that had been obscuring
his doormat and instantly throwing into the
bin anything looking vaguely official or boring.
This left a threatening letter from the library
about a book Bill was sure he'd never had, and
a letter and invitation from his niece, Clorinda
Byron.

Bill's eyes grew wider as he read. The little girl
he remembered with the swinging red pigtails and
the tendency to get stuck up trees was apparently
grown-up, and no longer interested in trees. She
was getting married next month, to a Malise

Madison, and would Bill and his family like to come to the wedding?

Malise Madison? What kind of a name was that? Bill wasn't even sure if he knew how to pronounce the name of his future nephew-in-law, and he certainly didn't want to drag all the Gonks along to some poky little church to throw rice at him.

Where were they supposed to go?

St Henry, Gordon and Bennett's Church,
Little Problem,
Lock-Jaw,
Near Chichester.

No thank you, Bill thought to himself, tracing the lovebirds on the invite with his finger. The wedding would be six snivelling bridesmaids five hacked-off aunties four beat-up Minis three drunken waiters two hymnals only and a gold-plated ring, made up to look like *Dynasty*.

Bill shuddered, and put the invitation and letter carefully back in their envelope. Tenderly he rammed the envelope behind an egg-box dinosaur on the mantelpiece, dating from the

Josh-at-nursery-school era, and forgot about it. He wasn't going and that was that.

Three weeks later, Carol was snacking on a slice of Morag's now quite alarmingly long-lived bread and 'tidying up' around the mantelpiece; a phrase she liked to employ when hitting cushions and dusting ornaments. With a careless flick she knocked the head off the egg-box dinosaur. Immediately, great waves of guilt broke over her. It was just as she was mentally kicking her shoes off and struggling into a life-jacket that she noticed the letter and invite. She read through them slowly.

'Bill,' she called. 'Bill, have you seen this letter about the wedding?'

'What wedding?' asked Bill, coming into the room.

'Clorinda's,' Carol said, absently putting the dinosaur's head on the end of its tail. 'Apparently she's marrying some bloke called Malice in a treble-barrelled church near Chichester.'

'Oh yes,' Bill said, 'I remember now. Sounds awful, doesn't it?'

'I don't think so,' Carol mushed. 'It sounds really cute and sweet. Why didn't you tell me?'

'Cute?' Bill repeated. 'How can a church be cute? It's twelve hundredweight of stone and pulpit. How can it be cute?'

'Oh, you know,' Carol said, wrinkling up her nose. 'Sort of, well, romantic then.'

'Romantic?' Bill asked, amazed. 'Romantic? A draughty old building with six hundred dead people camped outside is romantic? I take it you didn't appreciate our honeymoon in Whernside then? I should have taken you to Transylvania to get you in the mood, should I?'

'Oh Bill, don't start that again,' Carol said wearily. 'I've told you a hundred times, the honeymoon was lovely, I've no complaints.'

'You had plenty at the time,' Bill snapped. 'You kept moaning about my bloody fishing rod, and you never liked my keep-net in the bathroom, did you?'

'Well,' Carol said reluctantly, 'it was a bit smelly, but—'

'Ah-ha, I've got you to admit it now, at last!' Bill crowed. 'It took fifteen years but I finally did it! I saw you moping around in the lobby,' he said. 'I saw you coming into the room with a hanky over your nose. It was the smell of the rivers, Carol, the smell of the lakes and streams.'

'It was the smell of dead rotting fish more like,' Carol argued, 'and you never told me you had a tin of maggots in your wicker fishing box, did you? I thought you' d bought a picnic for us to eat the next day; there was a flask in there and stuff. I was just putting in a paper twist of salt and pepper when the lid came off the tin and they went all over my foot.'

'Well, if we're bringing up old grudges,' Bill said, getting worked up, 'there was no need for you to bring your cat, was there? It just sat on the bedside table and looked at me. Just looked. It put me right off, I can tell you.'

'How dare you slander the name of Meepo!' Carol shouted, cheeks reddening. 'She only died twelve years ago, and here you are being horrid about her! She was part of the family, I had to bring her.'

'Your mother is part of the family, but you didn't bring her,' Bill said evilly.

'And you would have preferred my mother sitting on the bedside table looking at you?' Carol demanded.

Bill suppressed an involuntary shudder. 'That's beside the point,' he said. 'What is the point?' Carol asked.

'I don't know, what is the point?' Bill asked. 'Of anything? Why did we bother getting married? Why did you bring your cat? Why didn't you bring a litter-tray? And why was it *me* who had to take the damned cat out in the middle of the night when it wanted to go? Perennial questions that are never likely to get an answer, eh, dear?'

'Well, I wasn't too keen on your fishing stuff either,' Carol countered, 'but I managed to cope with the obnoxious smell and the shuffling noises from the bottom of your box for the weekend, and I don't *moan* about it all the time.'

'You didn't have to take my rod-rest out on to the streets at two o'clock in the morning,' Bill snapped.

'You didn't have to endure a hook in the ear all the way down the M1,' Carol said, annoyed. 'And why you needed a rod-rest on your honeymoon is beyond me.'

'It was for my fishing rod, you ignorant cow.'

'Heartless beast.'

'Well, if you feel like that perhaps we'd better have a divorce then!' Bill shouted.

'That's fine by me, Bill Narmo.'

'Well, that's fine by me, Carol Narmo, or should I say Carol Rhodes now?'

'Yes, you should,' Carol said, taking a deep breath.

'Right.'

'Right.'

Carol left the room, slamming the door. She reappeared a minute later.

'So we're going to Clorinda's wedding then?'

'Yes.'

'Right.'

'Right.'

'—and we really have to go?'

'Yep.'

'She wasn't joking?'

'Nope.'

'And I have to go as well?'

'Yep.'

'Do you know any other words?'

'Nope.'

Morag snorted.

'Do you think it would help if I hit you?' Morag asked.

'Nope.'

Lily had found a new way to avoid arguing with Morag – just say as little as possible. 'You're no bloody fun any more, you know that?' Morag said.

'Yep,' Lily said, in immensely smug tones.

'And you're becoming unbearably smug,' Morag said. 'The RAF keep picking you up on their radars. WARNING: the next half a mile is contaminated with dangerously high levels of smugness, please use protective clothing.'

Lily snorted.

'What do you think, Aggy?' Morag asked, giving up on Lily.

'Hmmmmm?'

'About the wedding,' Morag said. 'What do you think?'

'What?' Aggy asked. 'Oh, the wedding. I'll just take a pile of books and sit at the back. It'll be exactly the same as being at home.'

'Except for the hats,' Morag said. 'No, on second thoughts, it'll be *exactly* the same as being at home. Lots of people overreacting, plenty of children being sick, and the most important person being ignored.'

'Oh yes, I do know what you mean,' said Lily, forgetting her new-found detachment and putting on an air of immense suffering.

'I didn't mean you,' said Morag, annoyed. All the Gonks were having a meeting in Lily and Aggy's room.

'Well, I look at it like this,' said Josh. 'It's a ride in the countryside and a plate of free sarnies.'

'But it's the most important day in anyone's life,' Lily said, aghast. 'The culmination of living, the peak of a person's emotional life; the only day when you could wear half the fruit counter of Sainsbury's on your head without any adverse comment, and all you can think about is crab paste sandwiches? No-one will ever want to marry you.'

'I don't *want* to marry anyone,' Josh said, sticking his tongue out. 'All that happens when you get married is you buy a poky little house and spend the rest of your life wallpapering and having babies. I won't ever get married.'

'Same here,' Morag said, sitting back on Lily's bed. 'I shall live in London and write my masterpiece, unhindered by male intervention. All you men do is lose socks and drink all the milk.'

'I do not drink all the milk,' said Josh, getting worked up. 'And if we're going to say the things women do, they hog the bathroom and lose the A-Z.'

'Look, it wasn't lost,' said Morag, as if this argument had been argued before. 'I knew it was in my room, somewhere. And look who's talking, Mr Oops-I've-Just-Lost-The-Last-Shed-Key.'

'Well, we know who lost the other six,' Josh said, all snide and snickerty.

'It wasn't me,' Morag said.

'It wasn't me either,' Josh said indignantly.

'Of course it was,' Morag said, slowly and carefully gaining hold of the edge of a pillow. 'You're the only person I know who thinks putting the key down the slot in the toaster is good crime-prevention.'

'It is until someone wants toast,' Josh said, tightening his hold on Aggy's pillow behind his back. 'Someone fat and always hungry.'

The fight ran its usual course.

*

Poppy was the first to awake on the day of the wedding. It was a golden, temple-stillness morning, and the diffused sunlight shone on Poppy's curls as she hopped out of bed and wandered into Josh's room.

Josh was half in, half out of his bed; his duvet was caught on the bedpost and trailing on the floor. Poppy sat down quietly on the carpet and watched him, thoughtfully.

Josh stirred, moaned a little as he snagged his toenail on the sheet, and settled back down into sleep. Poppy, not taking her eyes off Josh, walked over to his chest of drawers and took out all his socks. Silently, cat-like, she crept into Lily and Aggy's room and placed Josh's socks under a pile of battered *Vogue*s, stolen from the dentist's waiting-room. Then she went back to bed, smiling.

'Go and check the car, Bill,' Carol said, struggling into her dress.

'Don't you trust my friends at all?' Bill asked, ramming his foot into his shoe. 'He said he's fixed it, so why doubt the man?'

'Because he's one of your friends and because

he asked you to trust him,' Carol said, tying the nasty floppy' yellow bow about her neck. 'I trust Big Rod about as much as I admire his mother's taste in names.'

'Big Rod didn't have a mother,' Bill said, fishing bits of rubbish out of his trouser pockets and throwing them on the dressing table. 'He was suckled by wolves and taught to wrestle by wild apes. *That's* why I don't question his word.'

'Just go and check the car,' Carol said. 'To put my mind at rest.'

'It's not exactly doing double-time now,' Bill muttered, out of earshot.

'OmyGodOmyGodOmyGod,' Josh moaned, hurtling around his room. 'I can't find any *socks*.'

'It's gross,' Aggy said.

'I like it,' Lily said.

'It's gross,' Morag said.

'Well, I'm only lending it you out of the kindness of my heart,' Lily said. 'That and it's too small for me. You can take it or leave it, Aggy.'

'I haven't got anything else,' Aggy said mournfully.

Morag and Lily were standing around the half-dressed Aggy, debating on the subject of clothes. Morag was clad in a rainbow patched dress and wore her tartan dressing gown over the top. She looked as if someone had poured liquid clothes over her and they had solidified on their way to the floor.

Lily was wearing an ice-cream-pink skirt, a flamingo-pink lacy shirt, day-glo pink tights, puce-pink shoes, and she held a faded red handbag. Lily longed for the day she would be all in pink.

Aggy was dressed in an amalgamation of her elder sisters' clothes: a warped red and green cord skirt of Morag's, merrily patched with denim, and a baggy and rather sad-looking vest that had seen but couldn't remember better days. She was holding a maroon blouse of Lily's that Morag had named 'Variations on the Theme of Frills' some years back. And she was gulping.

Bill circled the car and prodded the tyre knowledgeably with his toe. The car *looked* all right.

*

'OmyGodOmyGodOmyGod, I can't *find* any *socks*,' Josh moaned, as he hurled himself downstairs.

'You could wear a cardigan over it,' Morag said helpfully.

'I've got a nice pink one,' Lily offered. Aggy's lip trembled.

Carol looked at the two dogs who were sitting so trustfully, staring at her, as she made sandwiches for the journey. Bob cocked his head to one side and whined intelligently. Max licked his bottom in a loyal way. They'd be so lonely ...

'OmyGodIcan't*findany socks*.'

'—I just know I'm going to be sick—'

'Pass another Murray Mint—'

'—purple dinosaur—'

'I still don't see why we had to bring the dogs—'

'Left or right at Newbury?—'

'Can't they put some decent music on Radio One?'

'Someone has sat on my hat—'

'GOOD.'

Carol was not coping very well with the hundred and one problems that beset her. She was regretting bringing the dogs, wished she'd had a pee at the last petrol station, and was beginning to understand why everyone in the whole world was so anti-wedding.

Bill's questioning was getting more and more frantic as a column of traffic built up behind them.

'Oh, left,' Carol said, hoping she was right. The page they were supposed to be on had been used to wipe up sick in Banbury before Carol had known they would need it, and Carol hoped a Woman's Instinct included navigation.

'Me want a sweetie,' Poppy said, from her perch on Morag's knee.

'Here, have mine,' Josh said, taking a break from making the dogs stay in the boot.

The dogs surged forward and trampled on Lily. Carol felt the first prod of a headache.

Fulk and Gabbo stared down at the first arrivals.

'I love a wedding,' Gabbo said, smiling soppily.

'I *bloody hate them,*' Fulk snapped. '*Bloody flowers.*' He sneezed again.

'I *bet you're the only gargoyle in the world with hayfever,*' Gabbo said, *with a note of admiration in his voice.*

''*S one too bloody many,*' Fulk grizzled.

'*You're a novelty,*' Gabbo said blithely.

'*You're a—*' Fulk sneezed. *Gabbo motioned him to hush, as more of the congregation were arriving.*

Morag stood in the doorway and stared around the interior of the church.

'Where are the vegetables?' she asked, looking behind the doors.

'What vegetables?' Carol asked, putting down Poppy and fiddling with her dress.

'The vegetables,' Morag said. 'The marrow and the turnips and the manky pumpkin with the dent in the side. The tatty bundles of wheat that shed all over the floor; the three tins of marked-down rice pudding. Where are they?'

'Only Harvest Festival, Morag,' Bill said, striding purposefully down the aisle and beckoning the other Narmos to follow him. They did. Josh followed last, employing a strange sort of crouching gait in an effort to make his trousers look longer and cover up his sock-free zone.

The Wedding March struck up.

Clorinda walked down the aisle in a dress that could have quite easily paid the Narmos' leccy bills for a year. She was smiling widely and trying to ignore the embarrassing sniffles that were increasing in volume from her mother. Her father, walking beside her, could be described in one word. Pinstriped.

He wore a pinstriped suit with a pinstriped shirt and a pinstriped tie, and his balding head with the few strands of remaining hair brushed over the top looked pinstriped.

His attitude was pinstriped, and if anyone asked him what his favourite colour was, he would say 'anything with a nice pinstripe'.

The congregation sat down.

'Dearly beloved,' the vicar intoned. A hush fell on all relatives.

'Want a pee, Mummy,' Poppy said, in a voice that carried to the deafest relative's hearing aid. All the hats turned in Carol's direction.

'I'll take her, Mum,' Morag hissed, making the

sign of the Brownie Guides. 'My good deed for the day and all that.'

Carol nodded, and leant back in her pew as Morag and Poppy stumbled past and out of the church.

Morag propped herself up against the church wall, and grinned. The extra pop she'd fed Poppy on the way down hadn't been wasted. Poppy struggled with her knickers on top of Mrs Peyton-Price's final resting place.

'Poppy!' Morag hissed in alarm. 'Not there!'

Poppy moved off sideways, knickers around her ankles, and peed on a clump of daisies.

'Oh *yes*,' Morag grinned, shaking hands with herself. 'Truly, I am a genius. The face of a bunny rabbit, the body of a hippo, the wit of an angry crocodile and the brains of a top-heavy weasel. Well done, Morag. Give yourself five.' She smiled indulgently at her little sister.

Poppy pulled up her knickers, picked one of the daisies and gave it to Morag.

'Poppy,' she said, sniffing the air, 'would you like to come on a little walk with me around this charming rustic church, and admire its architecture?'

Poppy grinned.

'I wish they'd take their bloody flowers with them,' Fulk moaned, as another sneeze sent small fragments of him plummeting to the floor. 'They just leave them here and it's not very considerate.' He gave a sniff.

'It's just unlucky about your arms,' Gabbo consoled.

'You mean the ones I haven't got?' Fulk said.

'The very ones,' Gabbo said cheerfully. 'It's a bit messy, isn't it, sneezing with no arms.'

'Yes, it can get a little damp,' Fulk said, with artificial breeziness. 'Ideal condition for growing lichens and moss, though, of which I have plenty. I should say I'm probably a lichenologist's dream—'

'A veritable gargoyleologist's delight,' Gabbo added happily.

'And you're most probably a—' Fulk sneezed.

It was cold, wet, and very late. Morag, Lily, Josh and Aggy were pushing the Cortina through the deserted car-park. Morag was whistling 'It's a Long Way to Tipperary' with manic cheeriness.

Carol was sitting on the back seat with Poppy, picking over a bowl of Twiglets. The two dogs had their noses pressed up against the back window and were panting smugly.

Bill poked his head out of the driver's window. 'Faster!' he bellowed.

Morag changed her whistle from 'It's a Long Way to Tipperary' to 'Colonel Bogey'.

Bill was in a chainsaw-usingly bad mood, and most of the skin from his knuckles was missing. His temper had escalated further when the dogs had escaped from the car and rolled in fox poo.

Poppy took great delight in saying, 'Urgh, wot dat smell?' every few minutes.

'You're going slower than the rest of us, Josh,' Lily said, glancing sideways at her brother. Josh modified his hiding-the-bare-ankles stagger slightly.

The motor started, and the Gonks swarmed into the car, grabbing as many Twiglets as they could as they passed Carol.

'That's it,' Bill said with iron resolve as they drove home. 'This car is No More.'

CHAPTER SEVEN
The Bat

Wolverhampton Train Station in summer. It's quite nice, actually: three day-glo orange bins, a burgundy newspaper kiosk, a couple of empty Coke cans and the odd train. A group of students huddle at the dry end of the platform in a soggy, Marmite saturated heap, their fashionable knapsacks digging into their shoulders, the rain dripping into their Doc Marten boots. They resemble little rain-drenched beetles.

The rain is pouring down, venomous in its attempt to wash away the concrete; pounding on the nasty, cheap benches with the middles ripped out; trying to cry away the litter and the smoke and the greyness.

The tannoy is broken and, as the train pulls into the station with its hypnotic whir, all the wet beetles scuttle forward hopefully.

It is not their train.

They seep back, disappointed.

An angered squawk sends the porter scurrying from his little hut towards the train, but he is too late, as a door is flung open and a leg clad in dark green, scratchy wool trousers is put on the ground in much the same way Queen Victoria would have alighted if she were alive and inclined to wear that sort of thing.

Denis, a promising art student, peeked out from under his dripping hood, took note of the legs' owner with the habit of his artistic training and, for years afterwards, particularly following vicious curries and promiscuous oysters, wished he hadn't.

A purple tartan jacket, worn over a vermillion shirt, was ornamented in places with various wild animals leaping in various directions. A string of pearls counterset beautifully the burnt-ochre tam-o'-shanter with pom-pom on a thread. Both lumpy tan suitcases clashed with everything.

The face resembled a particularly weathered gargoyle, with the added bonus of an unhealthy dose of the holier-than-thous ingrained into its countenance through the years.

It was female.

It was moving in his direction.

It was the Bat.

Josh was slumped in his room, bending plasticine animals into rude positions. It was a restless day: it seemed unwilling to admit it was Monday, felt like it was made out of congealed grey flannel, and tasted dirty yellow.

Josh had tried reading, but the words had not been in a friendly mood. They had mooched off the page, muttering about 'meeting their mates at a football match' and 'promised lifts'. He had tried watching the telly, but there were only old black-and-white films on, with lots of people called Celia telling Johnny to do it for her sake.

It was one of *those* days.

'Yew. Yew there. What are you doing?'

'Um, waiting for a train,' Denis answered,

wondering if he might be slightly foolish in doing so.

'Well,' said the Bat, in a manner that conveyed the utmost distaste. 'Really.' She retreated into her mind for a minute and came up choking, metaphorically speaking.

'Tell me, where does one find a tixi around here?' she asked, rearranging the paisley shawl draped around her shoulders.

'A what?' Denis asked desperately, wishing he'd walked to Manchester instead.

'A tixi, my laddie, a tixi. Are you devoid of comprehension?'

'Well, he is a student,' one of his best friends said, from the relative safety of distance.

'Ah, there's the porter,' the Bat said, sighting him and stiffening. 'Porter! Hey, porter—!'

Denis sat on the edge of the broken bench, under a very persistent drip, and wondered whether the Bat was a hallucination or for real.

John the Taxi, as he was known locally, was sitting in the tool of his trade, Bertha, eating a pork and pickle sandwich and listening to Country and Western on the radio. Apart from the odd lapse in musical taste he was a nice man, and didn't deserve what happened next.

A ring-encrusted finger tapped the window next to his head, and a face reminiscent of a cauliflower with an attitude problem mouthed the words, 'Open the door.'

John opened the door and continued eating his sandwich. The Bat got in.

'Rope Street,' she said. The harrassed porter dumped her luggage in the boot of the taxi and went back to his little hut as fast as his shrunken trousers would let him.

John maintained a steady rhythm with his jaws, and didn't blink.

The Bat tightened her lips and rapped on the glass that separated them.

'Rope Street,' she said, irritably.

John didn't move, and chewed a crust thoughtfully.

The Bat pushed back the glass partition and poked his shoulder.

'Now look here, young man, I've been sitting here waiting for over a minute. Take me to Rope Street and – don't smile at me like that!'

John looked at his watch, slowly. A small piece

of pickle escaped from his sandwich and fell on to the gear stick. He turned to the Bat.

'Look, darlin', I'm on me dinner break and I've got seventy-six seconds left, so if you'll just sit there nice and quiet, I'll finish me sarnie. Then I'll take you to Rope Street.' He took another bite of his sandwich.

The Bat fumed silently.

Josh threw a purple sheep into the empty ice-cream tub from whence it came, and sat on his hands on the edge of his bed. He got the idea that the sheep, the ice-cream tub, the bed, all wanted to be somewhere else. And as for his bedroom ...

The floor often looked as though it had a hangover, although that might be something to do with the nasty carpet. Whenever Josh came into the room in a hurry, the walls always looked as though they had just left a particularly good party and had been sorry to go.

'... and that's the brewery; been there since before the war and I don't know but there's some of the original hops in the bottom of the vats. Me and me mates have single-handedly kept that place open, and the amount of bitter I've supped over the years it's a wonder the canal over the road from the Wheel and Clamp hasn't overflowed, if you know what I mean. Oh, there's the place where the old theatre used to be; I had my first fag behind the storage sheds there, 'cos I used to work there, you know? Oh yes, I met all the great stars. Eddie Large gave me a fiver for putting his mike in the right place; he's a genuine bloke all right. I had a pint with him and he's genuine all right. Yep, that piece of ground holds good ole memories.'

'Am I supposed to be inspired?' the Bat asked caustically.

'And see that big block o' flats ower there?' John continued blithely. 'I bought a sofa from two hippies there. All the tassels were unravelled and the brocade covers were tie-dyed, but it still had a lovely shape about it – and the smell! It was something different, I can tell you.' John smiled at the memory of it.

The Bat ground her dentures.

Josh hopped backwards down the stairs to see if it would annoy anybody, and jumped down the last three. He had just started to play psycho-hopscotch with the patterns on the hall carpet when the front doorbell rang. He peeped through the letterbox, and gave a squeak of terror.

The Bat!

She stood, in suspended animation, on the front doorstep, looking disdainfully at a pair of Poppy's boots half under a hedge, which were home to half the slug population of Great Britain. She did not look pleased.

Morag wandered downstairs at that moment.

'Someone at the door?' she asked, noting the shadow against the glass.

'Yes,' Josh said, very slowly backing into the front room.

'Well, usually when people ring the doorbell, they want to come in,' Morag said, starting to open the door. 'I mean, do I have to do everything myself? I am trying to write the world's Greatest Novel, an – Jeesus wept! Uh, hi, Granny.'

'Well,' the Bat said. 'Really.'

Morag scuttled off in the direction Josh had taken.

'Groundworm,' she hissed. 'Where's Mum?' This is her relative.'

'She's cleaning out the fridge with Aggy,' Josh said. 'Blasting the lower layers of ice out of the freezer with TNT; snaring roaming Greek cheeses with gin-traps.'

'I'll get Mum, then,' Morag said. 'You keep *her* occupied.'

Carol was sitting on her heels in the kitchen, a sea of greeny-grey gunk washing about her feet. The odd detergent bubble looked very lonely as it sculled around. A little lettuce leaf raft floated about aimlessly in the dirty sea. Aggy threw her pink washcloth into the murky bowl of diluted Ark and watched in numb horror as it threw its hands in the air and shouted, 'I surrender.' A great glob of margarine, stuck to the inside of the fridge door, giggled evilly.

A posse of renegade wilted carrots from the lower reaches of the salad drawer struck out with a firm breaststroke, and soon had Aggy and Carol surrounded.

'Throw down all cleaning implements and give in,' the little orange aggressors squeaked, 'or we will make life very unpleasant.'

Then Morag came into the kitchen to tell

Carol the bad news, and life got even worse.

Bill came back from his Very Important Business Meeting a little tanked up, feeling hot, bothered and very damp. All of Bill's business meetings took place in the Wheel and Clamp; he said the air was conducive. Actually, there wasn't much air in the Wheel and Clamp: cigarette smoke, beef fumes and Cheesy Wotsits smell, yes; but air, no.

Bill staggered up the garden path, one foot in each weed-border, and so was particularly vulnerable when the Bat steamed out of number twenty-seven, hitting things with her umbrella.

'Really,' she said, jabbing Bill in the stomach. 'Really. I never, well. Really.'

The Bat pushed Bill to one side and marched off down the path, burnt-ochre pom-pom swinging wildly.

'Wh'was all that about?' Bill asked, staggering into the house.

'Well, you know that money she lent us, to buy a new car with?' Carol said, sitting him down on the sofa.

'Yeah?' Bill said, fumbling around in his pockets for a cigarette.

'Well, she paid a surprise visit to see the afore-mentioned new car,' Carol explained. 'Only—'

'We haven't bought it yet,' the Gonks chimed in.

'And,' Carol continued, 'as soon as she found that the Gonks weren't at school any more, there was a godalmighty row.'

'She said, "Well!" fifty-seven times,' Josh said. 'I counted.'

'It's a pity she left so suddenly, 'Bill said, with the air of one about to impart wondrous news. 'Because – I've just bought the car!'

'How much?' Carol asked immediately.

'It's a Volkswagen caravanette,' Bill said, shiftily ignoring Carol. 'It's got a fridge and a little cooker and a pop-top roof and loads of little cupboards—'

'How much?' Carol asked, narrowing her eyes.

'—and a sink that actually works, and curtains, for every single window, and a Greenpeace "We Love Whales" sticker in the back—'

'How – much?' Carol said, with stubborn persistency.

'—and it's even got its manual, which is just as well,' Bill said, starting to look uncomfortable, 'because it needs a few things doing to it. Just tatting, that's all.'

'What, exactly, will you be tatting with?' Carol asked.

'Oh, the light doesn't come on when you open the door, the passenger seat is a bit mobile,' Bill said, squirming, 'the suspension, brakes, that kind of thing.'

'Brakes?' Carol asked, leaning foward.

'And we only seem to have two gears at the moment, both of which are reverse,' Bill confessed. 'And there's a few light patches of rust. If no-one bangs a door it'll be all right. But apart from that, it's an absolute bargain.'

'For how much?' Carol asked, returning to her original question.

'Um, seven hundred?' Bill queried.

'Seven hundred?' Carol repeated.

'Seven hundred, 'ish,' Bill said. Carol opened her mouth. The Gonks tiptoed away.

Sometimes; just sometimes, it was best to leave the parents to get on with it.

CHAPTER EIGHT
Lily and the Bat Correspond

Some two weeks later, a letter to Lily lay amongst the threatening ones, addressed in a slightly wavering hand. Lily took it upstairs and sat, cross-legged, on her bed to read it.

12, Meatpie Lane,
Bath.

My dearest Lilian,

It's the Bat, thought Lily.

As you know, you have always been, if not my favourite, then my favoured grandchild. As such,

I was horrified to hear that your mother saw fit to take you out of full-time education. I had always cherished ambitions towards you finding and marrying someone who would make his mark on the world, as you have so many points in your favour.

She means I look better than Morag, Lily thought wryly.

But now, with any chances you had of gaining qualifications which would lead to a university placing, where such people are, gone, I admit I am worried.

 Please let me know if your mother is doing this against your will. As you know, I am but an old woman . . .

'Pleurf,' Lily said.

. . . but I am quite comfortably off. I would be able to take any legal action you thought necessary. Although this would be a state of affairs I would deplore, I do have your best interests at heart.

Love,
your loving granny,
Priscilla Rhodes

PS, Of course I need hardly remind you that you must not breathe a word of this correspondence to your mother.

Lily sat for a few minutes, in silent contemplation. Then she took out a sheet of penguin-edged notepaper and carefully wrote a reply.

Dear Loving Granny,

Thank you very much for the lovely letter. It was lovely. No thank you l am quite happy not doing exams. I probably wouldn't have been very good at them anyway and would have ended up committing suicide when Morag passed fifteen GCSEs (Ha ha a joke).

Morag said that she won't ever bother doing them (the exams), but my friend, Louise, says you can do Open University ones and I asked Mum and she said I could and I probably will. I would like to go to Open University, but only for the parties. I hear they have lots of illegal parties. I would like that.

Thank you very much anyway.

Love,

Lily

*PS, Had I known you were comfortably well off
I would have kicked up more fuss about the boxed
handkerchief set last Christmas.*

CHAPTER NINE
Scotland the Brave

'You see that wonder of modem science out there,' Bill said, pointing at the Volky through the window.

'What, old Vorsprung Durch Knackered?' Carol asked, not looking up from her book.

'It's calling me, Carol, it's calling me,' Bill continued, ignoring her. 'Do you know what it's saying?'

'Probably, "Heeeeeeeelp!"' Morag said from the bright orange pouffe she was sitting on. 'Probably, "I've got no rooooof."'

'It has got a roof,' Bill said, bristling. 'A few holes in the pop-top canvas are to be expected.'

'Well, what's it calling to you, Dad?' Lily asked, in a mood to patronize.

'It's saying, "The world can be yours." It's saying, "With me, you could park on a beach and wake up in the morning with the ocean as your front garden,"' Bill said, getting up from the sofa and starting to pace around. 'It's saying, "Let's go on holiday."'

'I don't want to go on holiday,' Lily said immediately. 'Wherever you go, the rain is always cold and wet and the Coke is seventy pence a glass. At least if we stay at home we won't get lost down some poky little lane.'

'Quite frankly, I'd rather share an oxygen tank with Bernard Manning than go on holiday,' Morag added. 'Holidays are a descent into an uncivilized world. Anyway, we always argue when we go on holiday.'

'We argue wherever we go,' Carol said, still not looking up from her book.

'We could go to Devon,' Bill said, turning to Carol, trying to raise some enthusiasm. 'C'mon, we'll vote on it. Who wants to go to Devon, run on beaches by the moonlight – that sort of thing?'

Bill put his hand up. No-one else did.

'Put your hand up if you want to live in a tin on wheels, poo by the side of the road and relinquish the late-night film on Channel Four!' Morag cried.

Again, no-one except Bill put their hand up.

And so, with it clear that no-one, except Bill, wanted to go on holiday, and that if they did, which they didn't, by default they would go to Devon, it's easy to see why, by ten o'clock that night, all the Narmos were in the Volky and batting up the M6 towards Scotland.

'There's Glasgow!' said Bill at half-past midnight.

'Still in Glasgow,' he said, half an hour later.

'A bit more of Glasgow for you all,' at twenty to two in the morning.

'In the suburbs now,' at quarter-past three.

'This *must* be the bloody suburbs by now,' at half-four.

'Well, that was Glasgow, kiddies,' Bill said at half-past five in the morning, as yellow sun crept into the sky and stained the pink clouds burnt-gold. 'Big, isn't it?'

*

Day One of the Narmo Holiday
It rained.

The Gonks spent all their time in the Volky, reading the Observer's *Guide to Spotting Birds*, the only book in the van, and arguing in loud voices.

Bill found out that he'd left his boots in Wolverhampton where, by a cruel twist of fate, it was the hottest day since a caveman stuck his head out of his cave and said 'Bloody hell, it's hot.' As the Scottish scenery was becoming more and more water logged every minute, Bill was confined to the van.

'I don't know why we ever came,' Lily moaned, hunched up, and avoiding drips by moving her head around erratically, in the style of a frightened mongoose.

'It's a holiday. Bloody enjoy yourself,' Bill growled.

'Have we nothing else to read?' Morag complained, hurling the Observer's *Guide to Spotting Birds* across the cramped and steamed-up interior of the Volky. It landed on a pile of folded sleeping bags. They slowly fell off the seat, out of the sliding door and into the awning that was pegged on to the side of the Volky. They knocked the small pan of scrambled eggs off the little calor gas burner, and extinguished the flame.

'Morag!' Carol wailed. 'That was breakfast, dinner, and the basis of tea. Now what are we going to eat?'

'I, erm, brought some of my homemade bread,' Morag said tentatively.

The Narmos looked at the scrambled eggs, being greedily licked up by the cat and dogs.

'The same loaf?' Lily asked weakly.

'It hasn't gone off,' Morag said, shrugging.

'I'd say that was cause for concern,' Carol said, with an air of futility, as Morag carved a few slices from the loaf.

Day Two of the Narmo Holiday
It rained.

After dinner (of Morag's loaf and jam. The jam hadn't sat too easily on the bread. It kept trying to escape) Bill sat in the driver's seat, unlit cigarette in his mouth, fiddling with his telescopic rod.

In the course of his long love affair with fishing, Bill had lost three coats, gained a nasty nick in the ear which had gone septic, and half drowned Josh on one occasion, but never once had he caught a fish. He was still convinced, however, deep in his heart, that with a little Male Cunning and the off-chance that all Scottish fish had a death wish, he would be able to recreate a kind of Swiss Family Narmo.

Once Bill had caught a fish, he had no idea of what he would do with it. He had a vague idea that it gutted itself, tossed itself in bread crumbs and leapt into the deep-fat fryer with a cheery 'Hey Nonny Nonny!' and a flick of its neatly battered tail.

Sadly, this is not the case. For a start, any fish you care to mention has a skull that would put the crumple-zone on a Volvo to shame, and will steadfastly refuse to die. About twenty minutes later you'll have a towpath covered with scales, and be holding a requiem mass for the poor dead fish that splintered three rocks, half a brick and the end of a rubber torch.

Bill didn't really know what sort of fish would be about either, but he thought it would be reasonable if, in Scotland in the middle of the summer, he caught a few seabass, dogfish, whelks, eels, and the odd pike for tea.

He carefully Sellotaped the cork padding back on to the handle of the rod and looked out of the streaming window. He stiffened.

A large, camouflage-painted Range Rover had just pulled up in front of Bill, ruining his view of the sea loch totally.

A man with muscles reminiscent of eels in a pink bag leapt out of the driver's door with the sort of healthy swagger that makes people feel violent towards them. Out of the passenger door jumped a woman with blonde hair that looked unfeasibly immune to split-ends.

'Bill, would you like a marmalade sandwich for afters?' Carol called from the awning.

'Bread?' Bill asked distantly, still gawping at the new arrivals.

'Take this to your father, Aggy,' Carol sighed, hacking another slice from Morag's immortal loaf.

The new arrivals, Bjorn and Odessa, had by now assembled a very expensive-looking tent, fished six healthy, plump fish from the sea loch, gutted them, grilled them over an open fire, and were now eating them with a tastefully arranged salad and wedges of lemon twisted into the shape of the Sydney Opera House.

Bill found this very offensive. He started to pick the cork padding off his rod in annoyance.

Aggy crawled into the front of the Volky, handed Bill his marmalade sandwich and sat down next to him. 'What are you doing?' she asked.

'Watching them,' Bill said, nodding towards Bjorn and Odessa and patting his pockets for his Zippo lighter. 'Me fag's gone all soggy now.' He took the sodden rollie out of his mouth and put it on the wonky heater on the dashboard to dry. 'That was my last one,' he added in annoyance. 'How am I supposed to look sophisticated without a fag?' he asked indignantly.

'You could do what Morag does . . .' Aggy suggested.

Day Three of the Narmo Holiday
It rained.

Bill emerged from the Volky and headed towards the sea, his quilted nylon anorak absorbing and holding the rain rather than expunging it. The cigarette-shaped object nonchalantly dangling from his lower lip was, in fact, a piece of whittled turnip.

Bjorn and Odessa emerged from their tent wearing matching yellow wetsuits, collected up their deep-sea diving gear and yomped down to the beach.

Bill watched them disappear into the far horizon before squelching over to their camp and peering though the Range Rover window. Carelessly heaped up in the back were two jet-skis, some lethal-looking harpoons, fishing rods for every conceivable occasion and, balancing on top of a portable phone, a spotlight focusing on it from somewhere – a very large carton of king-sized, duty-free Benson and Hedges. Shining, Glistening. Not Bill's.

Bill bit through his whittled turnip in annoyance, and squelched back to the Volky.

'Damn,' he said, spitting bits of root vegetable from his mouth. 'Damn damn damn.'

Day Four of the Narmo Holiday
It rained.

Bill was frantically searching every corner of the Volky, looking for money to buy cigarettes. The initial surge of Feeling Good about giving up, albeit involuntarily, had been replaced by Feeling Very Very Bad, and all the Gonks were trying to keep out of Bill's way. This was very hard as they were confined to the Volky, the rest of Scotland being wet.

'Ahhh ha ha ha ha!' Bill yodelled. 'A penny!'

'You only need another one hundred and seventy-nine,' Lily said from her perch in Josh's bunk.

'Oh, shut up,' Bill snapped. 'I should never have had children anyway, I have monk in my genes. And stop fiddling with your nails.'

Lily stopped fiddling with her nails, and started fiddling with her hair.

'Do you want a cup of tea, Bill?' Carol asked, taking the kettle off the tiny gas ring. 'No, I do bloody not. Tea bloody tea, that's all we have,' Bill growled. 'Why can't we have coffee?'

'Because the dogs ate the coffee 'cos you left the lid off,' Carol said wearily. 'No coffee. Your fault. Dig?'

'My fault! Ah, I see. I see now. *Everything* is my fault! The fact we have no money is my fault. The fact Poppy put the cat down the Portapot is my fault. The rain is my fault. Morag's bread is my fault. Lily's *nose* is my fault—'

'Wassamarra with my nose? Wassamarra with my nose?'

'—plays with divorced people on BBC2 are my fault! Maynard Keynes is my fault! The M25 is my fault! Everything is my fault! Well, why don't you just kill me?' Bill bellowed. 'String up Bill and the world would be a better place! Is that what you're telling me? IS THAT WHAT YOU'RE TELLING ME?'

'No, I'm telling you you have to drink tea,' Carol said placidly.

'. . . if I died you could have a street party with streamers and, and, bunting—' Bill broke off here and started to gasp, 'I want a *fag*, I want a *fag*, I want a FAG.'

'Don't worry about your father,' Carol said, calmly peeling potatoes. 'He'll be back to his normal, good-natured self when we get the Child Benefit and some—'

'—fags, I want some—'

'Fags,' Carol ended. 'I think we'll be going home tomorrow, kiddiewinks.'

All the Gonks closed their eyes and offered up a prayer of thanksgiving.

'Is that my fault, that we're going home tomorrow?' Bill suddenly demanded.

'NO!' everyone shouted back.

*

Day Five of the Narmo Holiday
It *didn't* rain.

Carol cashed the Child Benefit at the tiny sub-post office in MacSpittoon, and wandered back to the Volky, breathing in the salty air and sucking on a humbug.

She hadn't slept all last night, planning how they would fill the van with petrol and be out of Scotland in three-quarters of a nano-second, but now she wasn't so sure. The sea loch gleamed a rich, almost edible blue with little flashes of bright green; and the sky looked twice as vast as infinity, and then some.

Carol wasn't sure if she wanted to go home at all.

Meanwhile, Bill was sitting in the driver's seat, waiting impatiently for Carol to return with a packet of fags, and getting more and more worked up about Bjorn and Odessa.

Bjorn had sprung from his tent at half past six that morning, and Bill had watched, bleary-eyed, as he strapped a canoe to his back, jogged down to the sea, paddled across the sea loch, landed on the other side, strapped the canoe to his back again and shinned up a cliff.

Odessa had come out of the tent five minutes later, dressed in a teeny-weeny bikini and a pair of hiking-boots, and started assembling what looked to Bill like a gyrocopter, but he couldn't quite tell as her deeply tanned buttocks got in the way quite a bit.

The Gonks, meanwhile, had Gone On An Adventure. This involved wrapping towels around their heads, finding a good stick to hit things with, taking lots of food with them, and getting lost a great deal. They had found a secret path at the back of the campsite and were busy exploring it.

'Nettles there,' Morag sung out, pointing.

'Nettles there,' the rest of the Gonks repeated.

'Brambles there,' Morag said, pointing with her stick.

'Brambles there,' the Gonks repeated.

'Impenetrable thicket there, 'Morag observed, pointing. 'Impenetrable thicket there,' the Gonks repeated.

'So you lot clear it away,' Morag said, sitting down on a grassy patch and taking the Observer's

Guide to Spotting Birds out of her pocket and flicking to the chapter on *Kites, Twites and Birds of the Night*. 'And call me when you've finished.'

Bill was vibrating, dangerously near to breaking. He needed *nicotine* and he needed it *now*. He was being cool, he knew; chewing on a freshly whittled turnip cigarette, and squinting out of the window in a Bergerac kind of a way. He was waiting for Carol and, by God, she'd better hurry up.

Carol balanced over the cattle grid, still sucking noisily on her humbug, and took another sniff of the air. You couldn't do that too often at home, by golly. Carol had let her mind wander across the beautiful day, and was now pulling it back by its little silver thread.

Bill waved to her from the Volky and she ran over to him.

'Isn't it a lovely day,' she enthused. 'Sun and a little light wind, and the sea is so blue Liz Taylor could make contact lenses out of it.'

''Snot a nice day,' Bill mulched. ''Sbloody miserable day.' Carol looked across at the Range

Rover and Odessa, who was just tightening the last bolt on the beach buggy. It had the registration BUM 1.

'Oh, never mind, Bill,' Carol said. 'You wouldn't like to be a show-off like them anyway. Would you?'

'Yes, I would,' Bill said gloomily, climbing out of the Volky and wandering around to the back of the van. He poked a small patch of Polyfilla with his toe. ''Sexactly what I'd like to be. "Bill Narmo, professional show-off."'

'But you've seen how obnoxious they are,' Carol tried to soothe. 'You wouldn't really like to be like that and have a wetsuit for each day of the week, would you?'

Bill privately thought that if he had the kind of money that bought a different wetsuit for each day of the week, he would definitely like to be that obnoxious. Possibly he would have a canoe for each day of the month, and, and, and—

'Carol, where's my fags?'

'Oh, sorry. I forgot.'

'*Blergh!* Are these cooked? Are they actually *cooked*? I'm probably going to get raw sausage poisoning and die in my prime,' Lily moaned, spitting out little fragments of half-charred, half-raw sausage.

'Oh, sor-*ry*,' Morag said.

The Gonks had made their way up the newly cleared path, turned a corner and found the wide ocean rather than the sea loch. It shone like a piece of green cellophane with blue light under it, and mirrored the lazy white clouds that had no particular place to go. To celebrate the finding of this new Eden, the Gonks had lit a campfire with Bill's stolen lighter, and started to tenderly burn sausages on long sticks.

'What's for afters?' Josh asked, throwing his empty stick into a thicket.

'Don't know,' Morag said, standing up and brushing from her skirt the bits of sausages that were so burnt that even the dog had rejected them. 'Let's go back to the Volky and see what's lying around. Perhaps there might be a nice slice of my bread left.'

*

All was not well back at the Volky. Bill had exploded into a nicotine-starved rage about how thoughtless PEOPLE were and how brainless

PEOPLE were and why couldn't PEOPLE just do a simple little thing like buy a packet of fags.

Carol had shouted back that it wasn't her fault, she had a lot to think about, and why couldn't Bill take a little walk and get them his own bloody self?

Bill was just about to rip back with some scathing retort when the Gonks wandered back wearing the little wide-eyed, innocent look that each one of them had spent hours perfecting in the mirror.

'Ah, the children,' Carol said to Bill in a meaningful way.

'I don't care if it's Angela bloody Rippon. I demand the continuation of this argument,' Bill shouted back.

'Tough,' Carol snapped, wiping a few drops of the freshly falling rain from her face.

'Right then,' Bill said, jutting out his jaw. 'Right, then. If you refuse to argue, I tell you what's going to happen. We're going home, right now.'

'Why?' the Gonks whined. 'It was just getting good.'

'Bill, Bill,' Carol pleaded, 'you only have to go

into the village and buy a packet. We don't have to go home.'

'I want to,' Bill said stubbornly. 'I don't care if you want to stay here. I want to go home.'

The Gonks pushed morosely past the still-squabbling Bill and Carol into the van and sat down. They wound up the windows and looked at each other glumly.

'Typical parents,' Josh said.

'Bickering all the time,' Lily said. 'All they do all the time is argue. I don't know why we bother, I really don't.'

'I didn't know we did,' Aggy said, shaking the rain out of her hair.

'Well, we don't,' said Morag easily, 'but if we did, I wouldn't know why we did.'

'Why we did what?' Aggy asked.

'Bothered.'

'I see,' Aggy said, although she didn't.

The sliding door was shut in the middle of howling winds and driving rain, and the dogs had their travelling pills rammed down their throats. The cat hurtled around the interior of the Volky, mewling irritably.

The Gonk mini-rebellion of Not Bothering was crushed by Morag suggesting a game of Spot the Three-Legged Cow, which guaranteed a lot of shouting. Bill ground the gears and made sure that each bump on the cattle grid was felt by every person in the van. Carol sat stonily in her seat and glared at the inane Thing on a String that bounced from the rear-view mirror.

Bill drove all the way back to Wolverhampton through pelting rain without buying a single cigarette. He thought it was an effective protest.

Everyone else thought he was being very stupid.

CHAPTER TEN

Aggy and Alison Discuss

Aggy took Lily's library ticket from behind a jar of interesting rocks, and slipped it into her coat pocket.

Morag had lost her own ticket and 'borrowed' Josh's; Josh had 'borrowed' Aggy's, and now Aggy was maintaining the steady flow of things by 'borrowing' Lily's. Everything worked out in a Zen kind of way.

Bob, the least incontinent of the Narmo dogs, shuffled up to Aggy hopefully. Aggy smiled.

'Yes, all right, you can come,' she said. 'I'll just find your lead.'

*

'Farewell then, old friend,' Aggy said, closing the last drawer she intended looking through for the lead.

Bob whined resignedly. Aggy swooped to kiss his head, thought better of it, patted him, and left the house.

'Helloa there,' Alison said, shunting the Returned Books trolley away with her knees.

'Hello,' Aggy rejoined, dumping a huge pile of books on to the desk.

'Did you walk all the way with those?' Alison laughed, threading a spare paperclip into her hoop earring and starting to sort though the pile.

'No, I collapsed once or twice,' Aggy said, taking off her granny glasses and polishing them.

'That book you ordered's arrived,' Alison remembered, dropping her light pen and bustling into the backroom. '*The Tibetan Book of the Dead*,' she called. 'A little light reading, huh?'

'It's mainly about the living, actually,' Aggy said, lolling on the edge of the desk.

'"You'd better be good or a nasty colour'll get you when you die," as far as I can make out.

We used to have a copy,' she added, 'but Morag spilt Vimto all over it.'

'Not many people have had this out,' Alison noted, removing the reserve card. 'Do you want me to stamp it now for you?' she asked.

'OK,' Aggy said, toying with some elastic bands. She gave a little snort of contempt. 'Most of the books I have out no-one seems to have read much.'

'Ugh,' Alison said, struggling to make the computer accept Lily's ticket.

'I suppose it's 'cos they've been at school all day,' Aggy said. 'I don't suppose I'd want to learn anything if I'd been at school.'

'Mmmmurf,' Alison agreed, trying to stop the pious red light from flashing on and off.

'Gup,' Alison added, stabbing at various buttons on the keyboard. She gave a little frown, and looked up at Aggy.

'Is this your ticket?' she asked.

CHAPTER ELEVEN
The Jumble Sale

'Anything and Everything a Truck Can Unload,
Is Sold From the Barrow in Portobello Road.'
Bedknobs and Broomsticks

With jumble sales, particularly in Wolverhampton, this 'everything' can be taken to mean old *Reader's Digests* and a lifetime supply of polyester blouses.

It was a miserable late-November afternoon; all the buildings were so wet they resembled papier mâché models, and the only plant life still alive looked like overboiled cabbage.

All the Gonks were sitting in the Volky,

drowned in winter coats and woolly hats with obscene bobbles on. Carol was driving. There was a general smell of wet hair and aniseed balls.

Bill had been left at home struggling on a little ditty called 'Happy Menopause!' that would hopefully pay for Christmas.

'—take charge of Poppy, I don't want her wandering off and biting someone again,' Carol was saying over her shoulder. 'Make sure she buys sensible things; no more pink girdles, please.'

'Can't Lily look after her this time?' Morag moaned. 'Poppy always comes up to me with something small, black and lacy and says "Wot dis?" very loudly.'

'I looked after her last time,' Lily said indignantly.

'No you didn't,' Morag said. 'You *watched* her. You *watched* her savage a stallholder, you *watched* her tealeafing an emu, you *watched* her—'

'Shush,' Carol said. 'We're here now. We'll park round the corner and walk. I'm not backing into that poky space.'

It was ten to two. A small sparrow picked at a discarded hamburger and wished it hadn't. An irate husband left home for the last time, suitcase under his arm, and a small child picked up a discarded syringe and wondered what it was. A shaft of sunlight tried to struggle through the closely packed houses and tower blocks and fell, for an instant, on an old Coke can lying in the middle of the pavement. This was home to a family of slugs. Mother Slug was just regurgitating some mouldy newspaper she had mistaken for a frozen pizza, as supper for her seventy children and their friends who had come round uninvited. Father Slug was settling down with a piece of pizza he'd mistaken for an evening newspaper. The family ant was chewing at a slipper, and the kitchen clock ticked away quietly. Father Slug turned a page and noted a headline.

'Mother,' he said, rustling the pages importantly. 'Mother.'

'Woooolvf?' she replied, her mouth full of sick.

'It says here that there's been another massacre in the Allotments; over six hundred, they think.'

Mother Slug made sympathetic noises and passed the plates round.

'My brother Alan lives over that way,' he commented. 'I wonder if he's all right.'

'I expect he's fine,' Mother Slug soothed.

'I'll pop over and see him tomorrow,' Mr Slug resolved, and immediately felt better for it.

Unfortunately, he was unable to do any such thing, for at that moment a foot in a scruffy trainer came crunching down, squashing the can flat, killing all the slugs and making life very difficult for the family ant.

'Why do I have to *pay* for all her stuff as well?' Morag groaned, kicking the squashed can to one side. 'I mean, she always gets really *stupid* things and I—'

'Oh Morag, shut up,' Lily and Josh said in unison.

The Narmos rounded the corner, and the Old-As-You-Feel Club loomed before them. The waiting queue snaked around the soggy fir tree planted outside and resembled a Chinese dragon made of bobble hats and blue rinses.

The doors opened on the dot of eight minutes past two, the delay being caused by Mrs Harris's walking frame getting stuck in the Ladies.

A sudden surge from the back of the queue shunted those at the front forwards, causing several

115

malfunctions of pacemakers on the Admissions table, as fifty hard-faced jumble-salers shot towards them, folding down plastic rain hoods and struggling with their loose change at the same time.

Poppy found herself separated from the rest of her family in the panic and stood for a minute, wondering what to do.

Then she wandered casually over to the Bras and Jars Stall.

'Where's Poppy?' Morag bellowed across the seething hall.

'What?' Carol mouthed.

'Poppy? POPPY? P-O-P-P-Y?'

Carol signed back her non-comprehension. Morag sighed, and started looking for her littlest sister. She found her, busily stuffing black shiny nighties into her carrier bag.

'Poppy!' Morag said, pulling the nighties out of the bag and replacing them on the stall before dragging her sister away. 'Not those things. Nasty. Urgh.'

'They p'incess jessis,' Poppy insisted, trying to charge back to the stall whilst Morag held her back by her hood.

'No, Poppy, they're not,' Morag said, eyeing

with fading hope the rapidly diminishing heap of shoes she had hoped to comb through. 'Why don't you buy some toys? Look, there's still some left over there. Nice teddies.'

'Oh, hotay,' Poppy said condescendingly, and trudged over to the Toy Stall.

'No, not that either,' Morag said, taking the metre and a half high Smurf from under Poppy's arm. It leaked a small puddle of polystyrene chips on to the floor.

'I wot it,' Poppy said, lowering her brows to the top of her nose.

'No,' Morag said, 'it's nasty and urgh.'

'I luff it,' Poppy pleaded, her eyes suddenly filling with tears. A few worn-out jumblers who were sitting on the unsold sofa started to mutter in sympathy with Poppy.

'It's got things living in it and things hanging off it,' Morag said, regarding it at arm's length.

'It's my best f'end,' Poppy insisted, one fat salt-tear rolling down her face and landing on the floor in a sad little puddle.

Morag looked at her in despair.

Poppy gave a little sniff that indicated such a

weight of misery that surely her tiny body would break.

There was a pause.

'Oh, how much?' Morag demanded of the stallholder grumpily, rifling in her pocket.

Josh was standing just a little way from Morag and Poppy, and staring blankly at the Toy Stall.

He just couldn't believe it.

'Hello,' Lily said cheerily. 'I'm looking for a pink cardigan. Have you got any?'

'Oh yes,' the lady on the stall replied. She looked as if she had gone through old age and come out the other side, like a baby again. 'There's one down here. I knitted it myself, actually,' she confided. She dug the cardigan out. It was a soft pink, with little mother-of-pearl buttons.

'Oh, didn't anybody want it?' Lily asked, taking off her coat and trying it on. 'It's a lovely fit.'

'Well,' the lady said, smiling, 'I did knit it for a sister of mine, but she's gone now.'

'Is she, erm, dead?' Lily asked, buttoning up the cardigan.

'No, in the Isle of Man,' the lady said. 'But it's

the same thing. There's a matching waistcoat for that, if you'd like it.'

'Oh, yes please,' Lily said, tugging down the cardigan sleeves. 'Haven't you any children? Our mum knits things sometimes, and we always—' Lily was about to say 'wear them' but changed her mind, '—appreciate the thought.'

'Yes, but they're all quite grown now,' the lady said, bringing the waistcoat over. 'Scattered all over the place like ...' she gave the waistcoat to Lily '... like dandelion clocks. You know when you blow a dandelion and make a wish?' Lily nodded. The lady laughed. 'Perhaps I blew too hard.'

There was a pause.

'I, um, think I'll take these,' Lily said, pushing the waistcoat towards the lady. 'How much?'

'Twenty pence?' the lady asked. Lily nodded. She felt as if someone had started to laugh and then burst into tears.

'Thank you,' she said, not knowing what to say to the lady who knitted things for no-one. So she said nothing.

Josh continued to stare blankly at the Toy Stall. The base outrage of it all. The sheer effrontery.

And they'd always denied it. Well, it was a sorry thing for a boy to feel, but here I am, he thought, ten years old and embittered towards the whole adult population of the world. Mass conspiracy!

'Fifty pence?' Morag exclaimed. 'Fifty pence? It has no eyes, it has no mouth, it has no fur pile left. It has, on the other hand, things crawling around in it and a rather unpleasant smell.'

'Fifty pence is the price marked on it,' the stallholder insisted stubbornly. Morag had taken an instant dislike to her.

'But look at it,' Morag said, holding it up so all could see. A small stream of stuffing flowed out of its leg and on to the floor, and it slowly collapsed like the Wicked Witch of the West. 'Wouldn't you *consider* thirty?'

'Fifty pence is the price marked on it,' the stallholder insisted.

'But twenty pence of it's on the floor already,' Morag protested.

'Fifty pence,' the woman said.

Morag paused, flicking her last fifty pence around in her pocket. She screwed her face up.

'P'ese, Mo'ag,' Poppy said, widening her

oceanic eyes and letting trust swim across them.

'Ohhhhh . . .' Morag said.

Josh could feel he was losing his initial wave of antipathy to those that had betrayed him. He was no longer a red-hot coal of burning emotions in turmoil. He'd slowed down a little on his plans to kill everybody in the world and was now, in fact, leaking salt water from one eye.

There lay, on the table in front of him, the long-lost friend of his childhood days, companion in so many Gonkish ventures; his tail now chewed off by unknown dog's teeth, his foot strangely warped by someone else's carelessness. Josh noted he still had his red felt-tip eyebrows, endowed by Morag when she was nine. He reached forward and, with a triumphant cry of 'Clive!' snatched up his legendary purple rubber dinosaur.

Now everybody, a round of applause,
We're here to celebrate the menopause.
Though much maligned, I think you'll agree
It's better than having PMT!

Bill threw down his pen in disgust. It had been a

bad day for tapping into the inspirational sub-ether.

Carol burst through the front door with the rest of the Gonks in tow.

'Have a good jumble?' Bill enquired.

'Look what I got,' Carol said, with a triumphant grin.

She heaved her gem into the front room.

Bill kicked it, and it slowly unfurled across the floor.

'A roll of carpet with a hole in the middle!' Josh said brightly.

'Yeah, a twelve foot carpet doughnut,' Morag whunkered.

'Well, if you take up residence as Permanent Wit in the middle,' Carol snapped, 'no-one will notice at all.'

'Don't be horrible to Morag, you purple rubber dinosaur slave-trader,' Josh shouted. 'You gave him away to a jumble sale and you always said—'

'What?' Carol asked, colouring.

'You always swore you didn't know what had happened,' Morag said, cottoning on to Josh's gist. 'You always—'

'I may have forgotten,' Carol started. The Narmos slid into the argument like butter off a hot plate.

*

Later that night, Morag carried the drowsy Poppy to her bed. She tucked the duvet around the miniature body and smoothed Poppy's gilded curls out of her eyes.

'Good night, little Poppet,' Morag said, giving a warm smile. She felt very protective towards the tiny little child.

'Dood-night, Mo'ag,' Poppy said, snuggling down in her bed.

Morag paused just before turning the light off.

'Where's your Smurf?' she asked.

'Wot Smurf?' Poppy asked, her blue eyes popping open.

'The Smurf I bought you with the last of my money, instead of a new pair of trainers,' Morag said. 'Your so-called "best f'end".'

'Oh, he w'all smelly,' Poppy said. 'I pu' him back on the table. All his legs come out!' she said, widening her eyes.

Morag gave a weak smile.

Josh smiled in the dark, in the direction of Clive, and fell asleep.

CHAPTER TWELVE
Whoops Apocalypse

Christmas at the Narmos ... mad, bad, and dangerous to eat in any great quantity.

On Christmas Eve Carol was balancing on a chair, trying to pull a drawing pin out of the ceiling with her already broken thumbnail. In the process she was introducing Poppy to a few words she'd never heard before.

Last year the decorations had gone up on 13 November, fallen down the next day, and spent nearly two months trailing on the floor. Carol had sworn this year that not a single Santa would enter the house before Christmas Eve.

Josh was reading amazing facts out of *A*

Thousand and One Amazing Facts to anybody who would listen, and Lily was taking each glass bauble out of the Weetabix box, into which they had been carefully thrown last year, and wondering if she could use them as earrings.

'—and this man in Sussex apparently holds the record for the biggest sprout ever,' Josh was saying. 'It was twelve kilos ten grammes before the little crosses were put in the bottom. That is a big sprout.'

Lily held a bauble to her ear and turned to the rest of her family. 'Do you think this suits me?' she asked.

Everyone rolled their eyes.

Morag bustled into the front room.

'Do we really want stuffing this year?' she asked.

'Um, yes,' Carol said. 'Why?'

'Cat just ate it,' Morag said. 'I could make some, if you like. I've got a recipe somewhere. Breadcrumbs and stuff.'

'We don't have breadcrumbs in this house,' Carol said. 'We get bread, we eat it. It doesn't have time to crumb.'

'There's my bread.' Morag said.

There was a silence.

'Have we still got that?' Carol asked weakly. Morag nodded.

'Uh, just wrap the bird in foil and come in here,' Carol said eventually, vowing to broach the subject of what exactly Morag *had* put in the bread some other time. 'You can help decorate the tree.'

'This is a tree?' Lily asked, putting down her bauble. '*This* is a tree? Sorry, but I thought it was a lonely twig we took pity on and stuck in a bucket. I didn't know it was a tree.'

'Leave it alone,' Morag said, gently cuffing Lily. 'It was the last one in the shop. We couldn't hurt its feelings and not buy it.'

'Sentiment didn't come into it,' Carol said briskly, setting about the stubborn drawing pin with a Tommy Tipee feeding fork. 'It was reduced to one pound fifty with a tin of dented pineapple thrown in. *That's* why we got it.'

Lily snorted, and went back to unravelling tinsel from the runners of a miniature plastic sleigh.

Morag went back into the kitchen, braced herself and started putting the sausage meat into the turkey. Ugh. Putting your hand up a dead chicken's bum on Christmas Eve, she thought. I bet Charles Dickens never had to do this.

Josh wandered into the kitchen, looking for some small morsel to taste. He found the red-faced Morag and the turkey struggling on the sideboard instead.

'Turkey?' he said.

'Yes,' said Morag shortly.

'The heaviest turkey in the world weighed a hundred and twenty kilos and was bred in California by—'

Morag growled.

Aggy was in the dining-room, decorating gingerbread men with white icing and getting very sticky and cross.

'Go – on. Go – on. Go on! Please. Oh, come on, now. Please be an eye.'

Aggy threw down the icing bag and stared at her evening's work. Three gingerbread men had chins that had gone wrong, which Aggy had turned into beards, and two wore ponchos. One had a bow-tie on his nose.

Josh wandered into the dining-room and noted Aggy's gingerbread men.

'Recreation of Mont Blanc?' Josh asked, pointing at Aggy's rejection plate.

'Nooo,' Aggy said.

''Cos Mount Blanc is the sixth biggest mountain in the world,' Josh said. 'Did you know that Britain has only got the fifty-third biggest in the world? We always miss out on all the good things.'

Aggy made a vague gesture of threat, and Josh left.

Poppy replaced him, her eyes taking on their usual air of 'I'm just passing through so if you want anything, tough luck; but if there's something I want to fiddle with I'm here for the rest of the evening whether you like it or not, matey.' Her body was stretched as tall as she could make it to see what Aggy was doing on the table.

'I do,' she said, scrambling up on to a chair.

'Help yourself,' Aggy said shortly, shoving the plate and the icing bag over to Poppy. She watched with rapidly tightening lips as Poppy delicately iced the gingerbread men, giving perfect features to each.

'How do you do that, Poppy?' Aggy asked, taking off her glasses and polishing them.

'Just, me do,' Poppy said, shrugging slightly.

Mud, the Narmos' little grey and brown cat, was lurking in the bread bin, waiting for the turkey to be left unattended. She had had a perfectly dreadful day: Josh had trodden on her, Bill had kicked her, and Poppy had tried to trim her ears with a pair of pinking shears.

The breadbin had last been cleaned out in the seventies, and the residents had taken advantage of this. Mud had to put up with a senile seven-legged spider, an evil weevil, a hot-cross bun from 1983, and a malt loaf that claimed the Falklands War was still on and wouldn't surrender until told to by its leader, a packet of family-sized Penguins. These Penguins had disappeared under suspicious circumstances: the Gonks.

Mud ate the spider, and sicked it up under the sofa.

Now she was watching Morag wrap the turkey in foil.

'—few holes, but that doesn't matter. It lets the steam out, you see.' Morag nodded to herself and started to poke margarine through the gaping holes in the tin foil.

'Oh, deck the halls,' Josh said irritably, as a group of people in tinsel-strewn jumpsuits ran on with a basket of inflatable Rudolphs. 'There's nothing on the telly at all! Why do we bother to pay our TV licence?'

'We don't,' Carol said from the top of the stepladder, leaning at a precarious angle to pin a streamer to the light shade. 'We squandered it on the telephone bill. Pass me those balloons,' she added. Josh picked up the bunch: two round ones and a long one in the middle.

'They're obscene,' he said, passing them to Carol.

'They're festive,' Carol insisted, pinning them to the ceiling.

The Gonks converged into the little nook under the stairs. A curtain of discarded coats and jumpers hid them from view. Morag passed round a plate of potato cakes, hot and flat, all of them dripping with melted margarine.

'All fat marzerin does go up my nose when I bite,' Poppy complained, her upper lip adorned with a buttery moustache. 'Here, I'll help you,' Josh said kindly.

He took Poppy's 'griddle cake', and ate it.

Poppy was so shocked, she couldn't speak.

'Oy-yay, oy-yay,' Morag said hastily, swallowing a mouthful. 'We are gathered here to reflect over the year just past, make our New Year revolutions, and read out our special Year-Ending Poems.' There was much sniggering at this.

'No, no, it's a serious matter,' Morag giggled. 'We are, in a manner of speaking, putting the wax seal on the scroll of the past year, and as to whose mark will go in the hot wax – well, that depends on how good your poems are. Lily, your poem or thought for the year.'

There was a silence.

'Any thought at all?' Morag prompted her.

'Yes, I know,' Lily snapped. 'I'm just trying to find it.'

'What, your brain?'

'Shutup shutup shutup infinity shutup.'

'Josh—'

'I've got it now,' Lily said. 'Ahem. "Reflections on a Year Past" by Lilian Narmo. Ahem.

My birthday was dreadful
Another stupid blouse
Nobody ever gives me what I want,
    particularly at Christmas, and so I have a
    list here if anyone wants to read it—'

Lily started to fumble in her pocket.

'Josh!' Morag said, a note of haste in her voice. 'Your poem or thoughts on the past year, please.'

'Last year was, statistically speaking, the one hundred and twenty-seventh hottest since records began, but still amazingly humid,' Josh started, quoting from *Amazing Facts*. Lily snatched the book from him and threw it out into the hall.

'Thank you, Josh,' Morag said hastily. 'Poppy?'

'I wot anufer grikkle take,' Poppy said indignantly.

'Well, if anyone's interested in my own light-hearted musings on the last year,' Morag said, 'I thought up a jolly rhyming couplet, which I, um . . . forgot, so . . . Aggy?'

'I have a poem,' Aggy offered, chewing the corner of a sheet of paper with nerves.

'Go on then,' Morag said.

'Um, "A Poem About School" by Aggy Narmo. Ah . . .

'*My first attempts at prose*
Were twelve pages long and inclined to expose
The shoutings and cheating and beatings
   and fights.
The panic and shame and the ill-fitting tights
Of school.

'*We were laughing at someone who said what*
   we thought
Sneezes and sniffles and things that we'd
   caught
Hiccups and punch-ups and packed lunch and
   break-ups
Pinching and cheating and too many grown
   ups
At school.

'Um, that's it.'

Aggy looked up. All the Gonks were silent,

with looks of amazement on their faces.

'Do that again,' Morag said softly.

'What, my poem?' Aggy asked bashfully.

'No, not you, Aggy. Poppy. She just buttered six griddle cakes with her tongue.'

Aggy made a little noise in the back of her throat, and closed her eyes.

Half-past nine. The mock-log gas fire sends mock-flame shadows reeling across the mock-fingerprint walls of the front room.

The little twig in a bucket is weighed over to one side by the Sindy doll wrapped in a foil dress on the top. The mis-wired fairy lights are flicking on and off at distressingly epileptic intervals.

Three of the six streamers have fallen down. Most of the balloons have deflated.

'Oh, I don't know. Fart?'

'No.'

'Fireplace?'

'No.'

'Fingerprint?'

'No.'

'Ohhhh, um, flowers, fishing hook, flambéd in white sauce, faggots and peas, fettucine?

Stop me when I get close, will you?'

'Now now, patience is the key word, Father.'

'It's such a bloody irritating game,' Bill snapped.

'It's festive,' Carol said, pulling a nightie over Poppy's head.

'We all give in,' Josh said. "We're fed-up and we're tired. We all give in.'

'It's Foe, Daniel Defoe,' Morag said with a flourish. 'Well-known eighteenth-century novelist.'

'He's not here, is he?' Bill asked, twisting around. 'Nooo, no, no Daniel Defoe. How can you spy him if he's not here?'

'He's here, in spirit,' Morag said with a leer. 'One of his books is propping up the corner of the sofa.'

'Bedtime now, kiddiewinks,' Carol said, before Bill could start shouting. 'The sooner you get to sleep, the sooner you-know-who will come.'

'Who, Bernard Cribbins?' Morag asked in a mood of facetiousness.

'No, Farder C'ismus,' Poppy said, wagging her finger. 'He make all d'people happy and give eve'ybody toys and fweets—'

Carol smiled blissfully.

'—and cars and airp'ane and big boats and big shop,' Poppy continued. 'He gonna give me a big mount'in.'

'Everyone to bed.' Bill said.

'Pssst, Josh. Psssssst, Josh!' Morag hissed, beckoning from her room.

Josh was hanging from Bill and Carol's door, and didn't hear.

'Psssst. Sssssss, Josh, Josh.'

Josh swung absently.

'Oh, come here,' Morag snapped. Josh dropped with a thud and made a ninja-like chop at Morag. Morag grabbed him by the arm and dragged him into her room.

'What?' Josh said, checking under the bed for assassins.

'You know we haven't got any crackers this year?' Morag said, kicking him gently.

'Yeah?'

'And you know that chemistry set Granny Narmo gave us last year?'

'Yeeea-hhh?'

'Well! Just think of everyone's faces tomorrow

morning, all sad because they haven't got any silly paper hats to wear. Then – da da da! We produce our own box of crackers, complete with loo-roll hats!'

'Ummm ...'

The next morning. Early. The sun is still no competition for the orange street lights, some of which are faulty, or garlanded with tinsel from a few of last night's parties; all of which are making the neighbourhood look seedy, tiger-striped and run-down. A couple of birds are gargling in the straggly trees.

All the Gonks gathered on Morag's bed, clutching their bulgy stockings, sniffing at the outsides, guessing.

They knew, deep in their hearts, that this year would be the same as every year and nothing would have changed, but it was still exciting to wonder if, by an amazing twist of fate, there might just possibly ...

Lily tipped her stocking upside down on to Morag's rumpled duvet, and an orange fell out.

They sighed in unison.

'Same as usual.'

'This present's from the Bat,' Lily said, shaking the box violently upside down. 'It rattles.'

'Probably 'cos you just broke it,' Morag said, falling upon a red parcel with MORAG scrawled on it in biro. 'Who's this from?'

'Me,' Lily said.

'*Poo!*' Poppy shrieked, dragging a stuffed Winnie the Pooh from her shredded wrapping paper.

'You put a lot of Sellotape on this present, didn't you, Lily,' Morag said, sweating slightly.

'So it didn't fall apart in the post,' Lily said, opening her present. 'A book,' she said, with a plastic smile. '*Fractions and Decimals the Easy Way*. The Bat gave me a maths book. How kind. Here, you have it, Ag,' she said, throwing it at Aggy.

You can have the mittens she gave me if you want,' Aggy said, offering them to Lily.

'In the post?' Morag persisted, ripping at the tape with her teeth. 'You brought it down from your bedroom and put it under the tree. It hasn't *been* in the post.'

Morag ripped the last shred of paper from

her gift from Lily, and stared at it.

'A pencil,' she said finally. 'A pencil.'

'A very expensive pencil,' Lily said. 'I got it in a packet of three from WH Smith and you wouldn't believe the price.'

'Pack of three?' Morag asked slowly. 'Pack of three? Where's the other two?'

'I figured I could give them to you on your birthday and next Christmas,' Lily said happily.

'It hasn't even got a rubber on the end,' Morag said sadly. 'You could have at least got one with a rubber on the end.'

'They were twenty pence more,' Lily said, unwrapping her present from Josh. 'I couldn't have afforded a bun in the Ye Olde Copper-Plated Kettle then.'

'Thanks for the nail file,' Josh said to Lily, throwing it aimlessly to one side.

'Lovely raffia pot,' Lily said to Aggy.

'You can keep lots of things in it,' Aggy replied.

'Nice chess set,' Lily said to Josh. There was a silence.

'I'm only joking,' Lily said. 'It's a tennis ball, with all the fluff rubbed off.'

The family continued unwrapping. Morag opened her present from Aggy and Josh.

'A lovely pencil!' she cried. 'One for each nostril now.'

A general air of lethargy was hanging about by half-past elevenish. Morag beckoned Josh over to behind the sofa. He came, reluctantly.

'It's time,' she hissed ominously.

'Yeah,' Josh said, poking his head around the corner to watch James Bond.

'You're not listening,' Morag said, pulling him back impatiently. 'It's *time*. For the crackers.'

'Oh yeah,' Josh said, shoving his head up over the top of the sofa. 'It's that bit with the shark now,' he reported.

Morag poked her head up too.

Ten minutes later.

'You could see it was rubber.'

'Yeah.'

'You could even see the "Made in Taiwan" stamped on its bum.'

'And that's just Roger Moore,' Josh said dismissively.

'Anyway, it's time *now*,' Morag said, taking the box out from underneath the sofa.

'—and one for me,' Carol said, taking it out of the box. 'They're very clever, Morag. Old loo-roll tubes, aren't they?'

'Yes,' Josh said.

Carol pulled hers with Lily.

'Pity they don't bang,' she said, taking her paper hat out and putting it gamely on her· head. It fell gently sideways, rested on a ridge of her perm, and then floated to the floor.

'They should bang,' Morag whispered indignantly to Josh. 'I put enough of that grey powdery stuff in.'

Bill pulled his with Aggy.

'Heh,' he said, 'next year we'll see if we can buy you some of those proper bangy things. Very nice.' He put his loo-roll hat on the dog.

'Wretched things,' Morag said. She grabbed a cracker out of the box and shook it. 'Here, Josh,' she said, waving the other end at him. "Pull on this.'

'Oo-er,' said Josh, taking hold of it.

There was a bang.

An arc of grey powder shot out of the cracker and scattered on to the faulty fairy lights.

There was a flash.

The plastic Father Christmases on the tree started to melt. The tree itself gave off a faint tang of pine. A small flame licked at the feet of the fairy Sindy.

There was a little voice that said, 'Whooops.'

THE END